YOU'RE ALL I WANT FOR CHRISTMAS

A HOLIDAY NOVELLA IN THE
OF LOVE AND MADNESS SERIES

LONE SPARROW PRESS

KAREN CIMMS

Cover Designer: Garrett Cimms
Cover Photographer: Logan Noh
Cover Model: Sean Brandon
Interior Designer: The Write Assistants
Proofreading: Lori Ryser

This is a work of fiction. Names, characters, businesses, places, brands, media, events and incidents are either the products of the author's imagination or used in a fictitious manner. The author acknowledges the trademark status and trademark owners of various products referenced in this work of fiction, which have been used without permission. The publication/use of these trademarks is not authorized, associated with, or sponsored by the trademark owners.

ISBN: 978-0-9974867-6-6

A NOTE TO READER

You're All I Want for Christmas can be read as a standalone, but to truly appreciate the characters, it is strongly recommended that you read *At This Moment* first.

This book is dedicated to my readers.
You fell in love with Billy, Kate, and Joey,
and you weren't ready to say goodbye.
Neither was I.

And now these three remain:
Faith, Hope and Love.
But the greatest of these is Love.
—1 Corinthians 13:13

CHAPTER ONE

NOVEMBER, 1995

Kate Donaldson loved Christmas. The bright, twinkling lights and glittering ornaments. The sound of carols in the air. The cool, buttery feel of gingerbread dough between her fingers. The tantalizing taste of chocolate and peppermint melting on her tongue. And don't even get her started on its wonderful scents—cinnamon and sugar, fresh-cut pine, warm cookies from the oven, oranges studded with cloves, eggnog sprinkled with nutmeg.

Even as a child, growing up with her cold, distant parents, Kate had loved Christmas, especially as the month-long hustle and bustle melted into a gentle calm with the tolling of the church bells calling them to midnight

Mass.

She'd always been convinced that anything was possible at Christmastime. Miracles? Why not? Deep down inside, she still believed in Santa Claus.

But this year, despite the dazzling window display at Macy's, the hint of snow in the forecast, and the pungent aroma of roasting chestnuts, she just wasn't feeling it.

She shifted her shopping bags from one arm to the other and paused to watch a pair of Salvation Army bell ringers dance to "Jingle Bell Rock." The music blared through a boom box on the sidewalk.

She elbowed Joey in the ribs and held out her hand. "Give me some money."

"What am I? Your personal ATM?"

"I'll pay you back. I can't reach my wallet," she said, shrugging her shoulder so he could see her droopy purse strap.

With an exaggerated roll of his eyes, Joey dipped into his wallet and pulled out a five.

"C'mon. I can do better than that." She caught a glimpse of the thick wad of cash. "So can you apparently."

He fished through his wallet until he found a fifty, waved it with a flourish, then stepped forward and deposited it into the red kettle.

"Happy?"

She gave him an anemic smile. Was she happy? Not really, but it had nothing to do with the size of his donation.

With his hand tucked under her elbow, he guided her away from the bell ringers and down Sixth Avenue. "So what do the kids want for Christmas?"

"Everything."

He brushed a dark curl off his forehead with a leather-gloved finger. "Try narrowing that down a bit."

The purse strap slipped further down her arm, and she gave it a hard yank. "If there's a commercial for it, they want it. But what they want and what they're getting are two very different things. Devin's easy enough to please, but Rhiannon has her heart set on an American Girl doll."

"So. What's the problem?"

For someone up on all the latest trends, Joey Buccacino—stylist to the stars and her best friend since the third grade—was clueless when it came to kids.

"The problem is it's an eighty-something dollar doll, which is not only ridiculous, we can't really afford it."

"Yeah, but aren't those the dolls that look just like their tiny owners?"

A dog walker trying to corral five small dogs and a large Irish Setter jogged toward them, and Kate found herself scanning the sidewalk in case they'd left behind any early Christmas gifts for her to step in. She was already on edge. Walking around New York City with dog shit on her boots would very likely push her over the edge. It wouldn't take much.

"I already know what my daughter looks like. If she needs a reminder, she can look in a mirror. As it is, she's the only six-year-old with a mirrored vanity in her bedroom." She gave her errant purse strap another yank. "Thank you for that, by the way."

Joey chuckled. "My little fashionista."

Kate slowed to resettle her bags, the weight of which was numbing her forearms, and was suddenly propelled forward. She stumbled, but was able to right herself before she landed face first onto the concrete. Her bags fared less well; their contents lay scattered all over the sidewalk.

A man in a charcoal gray overcoat and leather briefcase slowed as he pushed past her. "Watch where you're going!" he snarled.

Billy would've decked the guy without a second thought, although Joey's glare should have set his hair on fire. She mumbled an apology to his retreating back and chased a canister of Tinker Toys across the sidewalk, trying not to mow anyone down in the process.

Beating her to it, Joey snatched the canister before it rolled over the curb and onto 34th Street. He tucked it into her FAO Schwarz bag, then slipped it off her arm.

"Give these to me before you create some kind of Midtown massacre." When the bags were settled on his arms, he tugged her out of the mainstream of pedestrian traffic.

"What's wrong with you today? It's like you've never walked down a city street before."

She tucked her hand into the crook of his arm and let him navigate them both down 34th Street and up Lexington.

"I guess I'm just used to taking up the entire sidewalk. When people see me coming with Rhiannon on her bike and me pushing Devin in the stroller, they usually get out of my way." She touched her head to Joey's shoulder. "But I guess I am a bit distracted."

"I'll say." He steered them toward a coffee shop on the next block and into a booth in the back where the aroma of fresh coffee, sizzling burgers, and fried food had her stomach growling. She was starving, so she ordered a roast beef club with extra mayo and extra pickles, a side of French fries, and a chocolate shake. Joey ordered coffee and a fruit plate.

When the waitress delivered their drinks, Kate ripped the paper off her straw and stabbed it into the thick shake. Joey's eyebrows were stationed just below his hairline.

"Let me guess. Either you're pregnant or you're trying to become a plus-size model by the end of the year." He tapped a packet of artificial sweetener against the rim of his cup, tore it open, and poured it into his black coffee.

He couldn't have known how much his words stung. She tried, but she couldn't keep the tears from clouding her vision.

"Honey?" Joey moved his cup to the side and grasped her hand across the table. "What's wrong?"

She yanked a napkin from the dispenser and pressed it into the corners of her eyes. The look on his face made it even harder not to break down.

"Not pregnant," she said when she was finally able to trust her voice. "In fact, won't ever be pregnant again, unless maybe you feel like donating sperm."

His eyebrows stretched closer to his hairline.

"What the hell? Romeo just walks into a room and you're pregnant. All of a sudden he's shooting blanks? How can that be?"

Thinking of exactly how that could be pushed her from teary to angry. Well, maybe not exactly angry. She'd moved past angry a few months ago. Now it was more like a recurring ache.

She sucked in a breath and forced the words out. "Billy had a vasectomy."

Joey's mouth dropped open, and he leaned back against the red vinyl banquette. "You're kidding. I thought you were going to have some obscene number of children in keeping with his hillbilly roots."

She was feeling too emotional to let Joey's critique of Billy's background bother her. "So did I." She twisted the straw wrapper around her finger and let it go, playing with the curled paper as she spoke. "Having had two kids so close together, and with the medical issues I had when Devin was born, we agreed I'd stay on the pill for at least two years before we'd try for a third. As soon as Devin turned two, I went off the pill. Knowing me, I figured I'd be pregnant the following month, but I wasn't." She crumpled the paper into a ball. "After a year, I talked with the doctor, and he didn't seem too concerned. And honestly, there were times when Billy would be away and I'd be wanting to pull my hair out with just two kids, so I thought not getting pregnant right away was probably a good thing. But then two years passed. When I still didn't get pregnant, my doctor suggested we run some tests."

She tugged another napkin from the holder, but this time, instead of dabbing at her eyes, she tore it into long, narrow strips. She tore those strips in half, and those into even smaller pieces. The repetition helped her focus on her words and not her emotions.

"My doctor gave me a clean bill of health, but suggested Billy get a sperm test to see if he was having some type of issue."

Joey threw his head back and laughed, startling her. "Sorry. I bet he wanted to cram for that one."

She fixed her eyes on his face, and when he saw she wasn't amused, he shifted uncomfortably and cleared his throat. "Sorry. Go on."

"I made an appointment and Billy said he'd go, but then he cancelled. Told me he was too busy. I made another appointment, and he missed that one as well. This time he said he'd forgotten about it. I made a third appointment, and I not only reminded him, I had every intention of going with him."

The waitress arrived with their orders, asked if they wanted anything else, and then disappeared. Kate nibbled on a pickle. The ravenous hunger from earlier seemed to have deserted her.

"That morning, he sat me down and told me he'd had a vasectomy." She shrugged, trying to appear a lot more cavalier than she felt. "He said after what happened with Devin there was no way in hell he was getting me pregnant again, and since he knew I'd just argue and try to convince him otherwise, he made an *executive decision*." She hooked her fingers into air quotes and changed her voice to express her extreme dissatisfaction with Billy's explanation. "He went ahead and had a vasectomy."

"Don't you two have sex like ten times a day?" Joey asked, looking confused. "How did you not know he'd had a vasectomy?"

Kate dropped what was left of her pickle onto her plate. "Because, he'd had it while I was still recovering from the C-section I'd had with Devin." The conversation she'd had with Billy was as vivid as if it had happened yesterday, and even all these months later, the hurt and betrayal felt as strong as it had six months earlier, when she'd first found out.

"He has no remorse whatsoever. He even insists that given the choice, he'd do it all over again."

She swirled a french fry through a puddle of ketchup and took a bite. "To say I was devastated, doesn't come close to how I felt. I couldn't even look at him. Honestly? I was this close to booking a flight to Savannah to visit my mother." She held her thumb and index finger about a quarter inch apart.

"Holy shit," he muttered.

She waited for Joey to indulge his favorite hobby: trashing Billy. But he didn't. His eyes downcast, he speared a peach slice onto his fork and slid it into his mouth, then followed it with a taste of cottage cheese.

"Well?" she asked, bracing herself.

His soft gray eyes met hers. "Well what?"

"You have nothing to say?"

Joey set his fork down beside his plate. He lifted his napkin, pressed it to his lips. He raised his cup and sipped his coffee, taking his time, gathering his thoughts. Clearly trying to tick her off.

He set the cup down and sniffed. "I think he did the right thing."

"But—"

He waved his hands, cutting her off. "Hear me out. I was there, Kate. I saw what you went through. I saw the pain you were in and how even the doctor and the nurses were beginning to panic. I was the one pacing outside that surgical suite, terrified that I might lose my best friend, or that she might lose her baby, or we might lose you both." He shook his head and his curls danced. "After experiencing that, if you were my wife, you'd be lucky if I'd even sleep in the same bed with you, let alone do that whole 'make a baby' thing."

She frowned. "Of course you'd say that. You're gay."

"Gay has nothing to do with it. It pains me to say he's right, but I'm saying it. I agree with him."

He couldn't be serious.

"Even though the doctor said my chances of having placenta previa again were less than five percent?"

"Yeah, even though. Granted, Billy should've talked to you first. I get that. But if you would've been one of those who fell into the five percent range, it wouldn't matter."

They finished their lunch in silence. Joey glanced over at her several times, but he allowed her to stew, which was exactly what she did. Not only had her irritation with Billy been rekindled, she was now upset with Joey for taking his side.

After the waitress cleared Joey's empty plate and her half-finished one and they waited for the check, Joey spoke again. "So is Billy's vasectomy what had you upset earlier?"

Raising her eyes to meet his, she couldn't help but forgive him. There was compassion there, and honesty. He'd meant what he said, but it came from the place where he held her in his heart. She could live with that.

She shook off the remaining hurt. "No, actually. What's been bothering me is that Billy's band might be opening for Rage on their Hired Assassin tour. They'd be starting out in New Zealand and Australia for a month, home for a bit, then they start the European leg, then back to the states for the North American leg." She sighed. "Between January and October, he'll be gone almost two hundred days. That's a lot of time to be alone, especially with two small children. And he'll miss Rhiannon's birthday. Again."

She took one last sip of her now watery chocolate shake and pushed it away. "I'm sorry. I'm just premenstrual or something. Everything bugs me this time of the month."

"Gah!" Joey cried, clapping his hands over his ears and looking more like himself. "I'm not one of your girlfriends. You don't need to tell me that shit!"

She poked him in the arm. "You're my only girlfriend. Deal with it."

CHAPTER 2

Billy sat in the parking lot outside the train station in Dover, nervously drumming his fingers against the steering wheel and singing along to Mother Love Bone. Kate's train was fifteen minutes late.

It was his idea that she go into the city, hang out with Joey, do some Christmas shopping. Although she'd tried to hide it, he knew she was upset about the possibility of his band opening for Rage on their world tour. It's not like he hadn't been on tour before, but this time, he'd be gone a long fucking time, and a big chunk of that would be oceans away.

Hoping to get her mind off the tour, for a little while at least, he'd coaxed her into taking some time for herself, while he'd spent the day playing dress-up and Legos, and trying to convince Rhiannon and Devin to take a nap.

He'd failed. Maybe the babysitter would have better luck getting them to bed.

The train's whistle rose above Andy Wood's vocals. He climbed out of the van and jogged up onto the platform.

Rush hour. At least he was tall enough to see over most of the assholes who clambered off the train ahead of her. When he saw her, her dark hair spilling out from beneath a knit hat, arms laden with shopping bags, he pushed forward, catching up with her before she'd gone too far. A smile stretched across her face when she spotted him.

"Hey, babe." He swept in and dropped a kiss on her cheek, then transferred the bags from her arms to his. "You got everything?"

Kate patted her side, feeling for her purse. "Yep. We're good." They made their way across the platform. "Where are the kids? Please tell me you didn't leave them alone in the car."

"Nope. They're running around the parking lot."

"Funny. I—Oomph!" A man pushing his way across the crowded platform slammed into Kate, shoving her into his side.

"Watch it, fucker!" Billy yelled, catching Kate before she toppled over.

She grabbed the front of his jacket in her fist. "Sorry," she called after the man, who had turned, taken one look at Billy, and backed into the crowd. She looked up and frowned.

"What? He almost knocked you over."

"I'm sure it was an accident. I think he was about to apologize before you scared him."

"Not my fault. He should watch where he's going. He's lucky I caught you, or he'd be the one on the ground."

Kate tucked a mittened hand into the crook of his arm. "My knight in shining armor." She batted her eyes up at him and laughed. "You're so predictable."

He grinned back at her. "Don't be too sure of yourself. I got Eileen to watch the kids, and you and I are going to dinner. How's that for predictable?"

CHAPTER 3

Billy studied his menu. Kate studied Billy.

This was not your typical: *"Hey, we've got a sitter. Let's grab a burger and chill for a couple of hours."* Nope. This was candlelight, soft music, linen tablecloths, reservations. Which could only mean one thing: Pernicious Anemia had gotten the gig opening for Rage on its world tour.

When would he tell her? During dinner? Or would he insist she have dessert and then pull the rug out from under her?

She watched him over her wine glass. His dark blond hair was pulled back, highlighting a strong jaw, plump bottom lip, sculpted nose. A lone strand of hair had escaped its holder, grazing his chin. He picked up his glass of whiskey and gave it a swirl before raising it to his lips.

"Know what you want?"

What a loaded question. She shook her head. "Maybe just a dinner salad."

He set down his menu and frowned. "C'mon, babe. You have to have more than a salad." He waved a hand through the air, encompassing the elegant converted mill. "Look at this place. The food's supposed to be terrific. You gotta eat. Did you have a big lunch or something?"

"I ordered a roast beef club, fries, and a chocolate shake."

He shook his head and chuckled. "No wonder you're not hungry."

She opened her menu, but her eyes remained fixed on his face. "Yeah, Joey wanted to know if I was pregnant."

His eyes connected with hers.

"It wasn't a very pleasant conversation."

Billy tossed his menu on the table and reached for his glass. "I suppose I was vilified again. Not that it matters, given that he already hates me."

She lowered her gaze and scanned the menu, but the entrees swam across the page. "Actually, he agreed with you. Said he would've done the same thing."

He set the glass down carefully. "While that means something, the only opinion I care about is yours."

"I know. I just wish it would have been a decision we made together."

"Would you have eventually come around to seeing it my way?" He didn't give her a chance to answer. "No. You would've talked me into another baby. You're my biggest weakness, Katie." He chased a drop of moisture down the side of the glass with his thumb. "I can barely breathe every time I think about how I could've lost you. We have two perfect kids. That's more than a lot of people. It's enough for me. It wasn't worth the risk. I know this still upsets you, but I don't regret my decision. Not one bit."

Before she could respond, not that anything she said could change what had already happened, the waitress returned. Smiling broadly, she focused her attention on Billy, ready to take their orders. Or at least his order.

He looked at Kate. "Babe? What're you having?"

The waitress redirected her attention with a smile of considerably less wattage.

"I'll have the Belgian Endive Salad and the Butternut Squash Ravioli."

She folded her menu and handed it to the waitress. "And another glass of Sancerre."

The waitress glanced at Kate's empty wine glass, and then foolishly, asked for her ID.

Of all the . . . She took a calming breath, but it didn't work.

"That," she pointed a finger at Billy and didn't miss the barely concealed laughter in his eyes, "is my husband. He's thirty. We have two children. The oldest is six. We've been married for even longer, believe it or not. Therefore, I am certainly old enough to have a glass of wine—or three." This was so unlike her, but she couldn't stop herself. "Besides. Your bartender carded me earlier."

The girl blinked twice and mumbled an apology. Eyes narrowed, Kate glared while Billy placed his order.

God help him if he even cracked a smile.

CHAPTER 4

The mattress dipped and Billy opened his eyes as Kate began her nighttime ritual. She squeezed a dollop of hand cream into her palm and worked it into her skin, running it up her arms and over her elbows. Her back was stiff, straight. It had been over six months since she'd found out about the vasectomy, and every time he thought she was over it, something would set her off.

Fucking Joey.

The scent of apples drifted toward him. She always smelled of the sweetest, juiciest fruit.

"You get Devin back to sleep?"

"Uh huh."

"I heard you singing. Funny." He chuckled. She didn't. "I'm the singer in the family, and he always wants you to sing to him."

"I'm his mother," she answered tersely.

And he was his son's father, but judging by her clipped tones, which he'd endured most of the evening, he wasn't about to point out the obvious; not when she'd likely answer with a remark about how there could have been more children, or remind him that since he wasn't around much, it was no wonder Devin preferred her to him.

She'd been so worked up about his vasectomy—again—that he still hadn't told her about the phone call.

One fire at a time. It was all he could manage.

Kate lifted her hairbrush from the nightstand.

"Let me," he said, grasping the brush. Her hold grew tighter, but with a gentle tug, he took it from her. Her back grew stiffer. He began to brush, slowly and deliberately, not bothering to count out the usual hundred strokes. He was more intent on getting her to give in, relax. Besides, he loved her hair. Shiny and dark, it nearly skimmed the swell of her hips. Just the feel of the silky softness between his fingers sparked a seed of desire.

Two- or three-hundred strokes later, Kate's hair snapped with electricity while her shoulders drooped and her head lolled to the side. And when he touched his lips to the spot below her ear, he could have sworn she purred. He tossed the hairbrush onto the nightstand, and gently rotated Kate's shoulders. Her neck was exposed, vulnerable, and begging for his mouth. He pressed his lips to the hollow of her throat and hooked a callused finger into the strap of her camisole, drawing it downward.

He positioned himself behind her. "Why are you wearing this?" He let his words dance across her back while he lowered the strap on her other shoulder. His hands circled her waist, and he lifted the silky fabric, sliding upward slowly, stopping when he reached her breasts. Her nipples hardened, and when he gently tugged and pinched, she squirmed against him.

He didn't want to go slow; he wanted to flip her over, relieve the stress that had been building in him since he'd heard from the band's manager that afternoon, but that would be a big mistake. Katie needed wooing right now, and clearly, dinner hadn't done it.

Billy lifted the camisole, reassured when she raised her arms without him having to ask. Then he eased her onto her back, and lay her down against the pillows.

He kissed the corners of her mouth and brushed his nose the length of hers, then along the curve of her jaw. With his hand cradling the back of her head, and his fingers threaded in her hair, he swept his tongue across her lower lip, capturing it and sucking it into his mouth. By the time his tongue found hers, she had pressed her bare breasts against his naked chest, a feeling he loved as much as he did the first time he'd had her beneath him.

Despite the niggling reminder in the back of his brain of the difficult conversation ahead, he dedicated himself to kissing her. It was her weakness and he wanted her to be receptive to what he had to say. She was breathing hard when he pulled back.

He ran his thumb over her swollen lips.

"Do you have any idea how much I love you?"

She blinked twice, seemingly incapable of speech.

His hand ghosted down her arm. When he reached her fingers, he clasped them between his, raising her arm over and head and pinning her in place.

"From the moment you stepped into my life, my soul recognized that I couldn't live without you. I said goodbye to you that first weekend, but I wasn't gone from you ten minutes before I ached for you. It was like missing a limb I didn't even know I'd had. I wanted you in my life, and I recognized early on that I was in love. Before you, I didn't believe in love, let alone love at first sight, but fuck me—there you were. And I was in deep, Katie. And every day since then, even deeper."

Her pupils were wide and her eyes the color of a dark, piney forest in the low light. He steadied his gaze. She needed to hear him and understand, once and for all. With his free hand, he hooked her leg around his arm and pulled it up, settling himself between her legs. Her toe traced a line up his calf.

"I was wrong for not telling you about my vasectomy and for keeping it from you for so long." Her foot stilled and her eyes narrowed. He dropped his head and kissed his way up her chest to her throat, over the column of her neck, until he reached her mouth. His lips touched hers in a whisper of a kiss.

"The doctor said the odds of what happened when you had Devin happening again were low, but they were still too high for me, Katie. One percent would be too high. We have two healthy, beautiful children, and we have each other. To take that risk to make our family bigger? I couldn't do it. I couldn't risk losing you. It's as simple as that."

The pained look in her eyes was raw and difficult to see. He rested his forehead against her shoulder. "I'm selfish, Katie. I couldn't live without you. I'd never survive. And what about Rhiannon and Devin? What would they do without you?"

The last few words caught in his throat, and he had to force them past his lips. In their previous discussions, he'd adopted a mask of false bravado—laying down the law in some phony macho, beating on his chest, I-know-what's-best-for-both-of-us bullshit, but not this time. This time he spoke from his heart.

Other than the subtle rise and fall of her chest, Kate hadn't moved beneath him. He didn't know what more he could say to defend what he'd done. Maybe it was irrational, but he'd done what he believed he had to. And irrational or not, he'd do it again.

He was still struggling with something else to say, when Kate's hands fluttered over his shoulders and into his hair. Soft lips brushed his temple.

"How can your words cut me so deeply yet still make me feel loved?"

He lifted his head. There was pain in her eyes, but maybe, finally, there was also a glimmer of understanding. "Because I did what I had to do from the depth of my feelings for you. What I did, I did from love and only love."

She cupped his face with her hands. This time it was her nose that traced his, angling toward his lips. Her kiss was soft, gentle.

"Are you asking my forgiveness?"

"For not telling you? Yes. For doing what I did? No. For that I'm asking your understanding." He waited, his eyes locked on hers. She shifted beneath him, pressing her hips into his. And his cock, which had softened moments earlier, sprang back to life.

She didn't answer right away, and he was afraid there was a chance she might never forgive him. Her eyes filled with tears, but he was heartened when she smiled.

"Consider it done. I'm sad that we won't have any more children, but faced with a similar decision about you, I'd probably do the same thing."

He brushed himself against the warmth of her. "Does that mean you love me, too, Katie?" He was aching to enter her, but he did his best to hold back for one more second.

"Of course it does. It means I love you with my whole heart."

There was no more going slow. He pushed into her, losing himself in the feeling. And even though he'd made love to her just the night before, for the first time in a long while, it felt like coming home.

CHAPTER 5

Kate stood at the stove waiting for the surface of her pancakes to bubble and the edges to brown so she could flip them. She felt Billy behind her even before he wrapped his arms around her and rested his chin on her shoulder.

"When will our kids be old enough to make their own breakfast so we can have morning sex again?" The soft hairs on his face tickled her ear.

She leaned into him, flipped the pancakes, and then wiggled away to pluck his mug from the drain board. She poured him a cup of coffee, and with a smirk, handed it to him. "How old were you when you started getting your own breakfast?"

He kissed Rhiannon's head and ruffled Devin's hair before looping a long leg over a stool at the counter. "Probably Devin's age."

She laughed. "Doubtful. He's only four, remember?"

Billy stared at her blankly and shrugged. She felt her smile slip as she thought of what little she knew about his parents—none of it good. When she responded, she kept her voice light and teasing although her gut twisted, thinking of a four-year-old Billy—any four-year-old really—having to get his own breakfast.

"You don't get your own breakfast now." She pointed the spatula at the cup he was bringing to his lips. "You don't even get your own coffee."

"Because you like waiting on me." She turned to argue, but was disarmed by his smile. Instead she chuckled and shook her head.

"Do you want pancakes or eggs?" She slid a pancake onto a Cinderella plate, drizzled it with syrup, and gave it to her daughter. The second pancake was destined for a plate featuring Buzz Lightyear and Woody from Toy Story. She smeared a spoonful of grape jelly over it, cut it into bite-sized pieces, and set it before Devin.

Rhiannon put down her pink crayon, the one she'd been using to color the Christmas trees in the coloring book Kate's mother had sent her. "I want pink milk," she announced.

"You don't like strawberry milk," Kate reminded her daughter.

Rhiannon looked at her with all the exasperation a six-year-old could muster. "I know that, but I want pink milk."

"I want brown milk," Devin chimed in.

Billy swiped a piece of pancake from his daughter's plate. "Rhiannon, your mother says you don't like pink milk."

The child actually rolled her eyes. "I don't like *strawberry* milk, Daddy, but I love *pink* milk. Pink is my favorite flavor."

"Pink isn't a flav—"

Kate waved him off. "I got this." She opened the cupboard and pulled down a box of food coloring. She squirted two drops of red into Rhiannon's milk and gave it a stir.

"How about you, buddy?" she asked Devin. "Would you like green milk? It's way cooler than chocolate milk."

His mouth full, Devin nodded. Kate did the same for him, then focused on Billy.

"What about you? What do you want for breakfast?"

He grinned wickedly. "I already told you what I wanted for breakfast."

She looked at the imaginary watch on her wrist—the only kind she'd consider wearing—and shook her head. "You'll have to wait about six or seven years. In the meantime, do you want pancakes or eggs?"

Billy stood and refilled his mug, making a show of it as he did. "Nothing for me. I'm not really hungry."

She parked herself in front of him, and tipped her face up toward his. "Not hungry? After last night, I'd think you'd be starving this morning."

His fingers caressed her cheek. "Maybe you wore me out, and I'm too tired to eat." He pressed a kiss to her forehead. He smiled, but it didn't reach his eyes. Something was bothering him. The dinner out wasn't all that unusual, but the fact that he had made the effort to secure a babysitter and had even made reservations when he'd never done anything like that before, had needled her last night. It needled her even more now.

After the kids finished eating, Kate set them both down in front of the television while she followed Billy upstairs.

"Want to tell me what's going on?"

The look on his face was guarded. "What do you mean?"

"I had a feeling you wanted to talk to me last night at dinner, but we got a bit off course." He didn't answer; he just continued getting dressed. Another sure sign. Billy would never argue or discuss anything important with her while he was undressed. She'd learned that early on in their relationship. It was like he was giving up some power if he wasn't wearing pants. He tugged a T-shirt over his head and then followed it with a flannel shirt that had been draped over a chair in their bedroom. She waited.

After he buttoned the shirt and rolled the cuffs up over his inked forearms, he sat down on the bed beside her, but before he could speak, she blurted out what had been bothering her for weeks.

"I suppose you heard from the tour manager and Pernicious Anemia got the gig with Rage."

Billy stared at her hand on the bed between them, and with his index finger, traced a path from her knuckle up her forearm, stopping at the edge of the her sleeve.

"Yeah, I heard from Alan, but no, we didn't get the gig with Rage."

Relief, peppered with concern, flooded her. Billy not being gone most of the year was a good thing, but there was a mortgage and plenty of other bills that needed to be paid. She wasn't sure how to react.

His fingers scraped against several days growth on his cheek. "We did land another tour though. This one's not as long as we're coming in late. The opener got fired, so we're picking up the last six weeks of the North American leg."

She wanted to squeal, but the look on his face held her back.

"What's wrong? Are you disappointed you're not going with Rage?"

"Honestly? A little, yeah. I mean visiting all those countries? Not to mention, Rage is a fucking awesome band. But I didn't want to be gone that long either. We'd have taken the gig if we'd been offered it, but it is what it is."

"Well, honestly, I'm not sorry you won't be gone for so long. I don't want to sound petty, but I like falling asleep in your arms. Sue me."

He smiled, but it wasn't a full-on grin like she would have expected with that remark.

"When do you leave and where are you going?"

Billy rose and stood at the window, looking out over the farm next door. "Tomorrow."

Her jaw dropped. "I hope to hell you're kidding." She hadn't even started decorating for Christmas, and other than what she'd bought in New York the day before, she'd hardly done any Christmas shopping.

"No. Not kidding."

"When will you be back?"

His shoulders crept upward and drew closer together, while he jammed his hands into the pockets of his jeans. "Not until the first."

The first? That seemed rather pointless. "Friday's the first."

"The first," he repeated, his back still to her. "Of January."

CHAPTER 6

Kate might have thought she could hide her emotions from Billy, but he knew better. Everything she felt or thought was usually broadcast across her face, from the widening of her eyes to the downturn of her mouth. The way she looked right about now, he'd say she was pretty much devastated.

And it was killing him.

Not once in the ten years he'd been a full-time musician had he not wanted to head out on tour. It's not that he was ever glad to leave his family behind, but there was an excitement that crackled just beneath the surface before a new tour. He loved what he did. And despite the roadblocks Christa Dunphy, his former agent, had been throwing in his direction since he'd fired her after what happened between them the night Devin was born, he'd still been able to take care of his family.

And he'd bet any amount of money that Christa was somehow responsible for the Rage gig falling apart at the last minute.

Kate blinked several times. "But what about Christmas?"

This was even harder than he thought it would be. He raked a hand through his hair.

The pitch of her voice rose. "Billy. What about Christmas?"

"Katie. Sit down, please?" He wrapped his hand around her elbow and led her to the edge of the bed. "I don't like this anymore than you do, but what am I supposed to do? It's not my band. I don't call the shots. If I did, I wouldn't have booked us to work over the holidays, especially on the other side of the country."

Kate lowered herself onto the bed. Her mouth opened, but no words came out.

He dropped down beside her. "I don't have a choice. For better or worse, I was counting on having a gig for most of next year. That's gone now. I can't afford to walk away from this—none of the guys can. As it is, the gig with Truth Monkey only lasts until mid-January. After that, who the fuck knows? Alan's scrambling to book more gigs, but even he was pretty sure we'd landed the Hired Assassin tour." Or at least that was what the fucker was claiming. Billy would have fired his ass a long time ago if it had been up to him. Just one more reason he wanted his own band. He liked being in control. If he was, he sure as hell wouldn't be spending Christmas in Southern California.

"Financially, we're fucked. You have to believe me, if there were any other way, I'd do it. If I didn't have two years invested in Pernicious Anemia, I'd walk away and pick up studio work for a few weeks if I had to. Who knows? If Alan doesn't pick up enough gigs after this tour, we might be done anyway."

"Can you fly home Christmas Eve at least?" Kate asked, her voice small, squeaky; the words making him bleed inside.

He shook his head. "The tour is booked for a private gig that afternoon, something for sick kids I think. We're off Christmas Day, but have a gig the day after. There just isn't enough time to fly across the country and back in one day. Not if I want to do more than sit on a plane or in a car, to and from the airport."

Kate listened quietly, and then just as he'd expected, she tried to make him feel better about splitting their family up on Christmas.

"That would be crazy," she said. "All that traveling to be home for less than twenty-four hours? I just don't understand why anyone would book a gig on Christmas Eve."

"Rafe Summerland, Truth Monkey's front man, lives in LA. Pretty sure the rest of the band lives out there as well. For them it's no big deal."

He watched Kate's face as she tried to process what he'd just told her. She took a deep breath, gave him a pained little smile, and stood.

"I guess we'd better get busy then. I have to run Rhiannon to school. I'll drop Devin off at preschool early. While I'm doing that, could you get the Christmas decorations down from the attic? I'll run to Lane's and see if I can pick up an artificial tree." She avoided looking at him while she changed out of her nightgown and pulled a sweater over her head. "A real one would be dead before you get home."

He captured her hand as she passed and pulled her against him. He pressed his lips into the top of her head and inhaled deeply, trying to refresh the memory of the sweet orange scent that was typically Kate. "I'm sorry, babe."

She buried her face in his chest and nodded.

CHAPTER 7

By nightfall, wreaths had been hung in the windows on the front of the house and the door, and the artificial tree was up and decorated. Billy would finish packing in the morning, but for now, he was stretched out on Rhiannon's bed, reading from the "Chronicles of Narnia."

Devin wiggled under his arm and tugged on a lock of hair that had escaped from Billy's ponytail.

"What, buddy?"

Serious blue eyes looked into his. "What about Santa? Will he still come if you're not here?"

A lump formed in his throat. He lowered the book. "Of course he'll come."

Rhiannon sat up, pushed out her bottom lip, and brushed a corkscrew curl from her forehead. "Yeah, but will we be able to open presents or do we have to wait till you come home?"

"No." Billy struggled to clear his throat. "You won't have to wait. Just promise me you'll leave everything under the tree so that I can see what Santa brings you, okay? And I promise, when I get home, we'll play all day, no matter what."

She eyed him skeptically. "Even Barbies?"

"Especially Barbies."

Devin had fallen asleep before Billy had finished the chapter. He kissed his daughter goodnight, promised her he'd be there to have breakfast with her in the morning, and then carried his son to bed. He pulled the covers up and tucked them under Devin's chin, then he bent down and kissed his warm, soft cheek, breathing in the scent of baby shampoo and fresh pajamas. Times like these were when he most regretted his vasectomy, but he could never share that with Kate. If she knew, she'd want him to have the surgery reversed, and that he wouldn't do.

With one more kiss, he pushed off Devin's bed and crossed the hall into his bedroom where Kate was plugging in the last of the electric candles she'd set in each window.

She flicked it on. "I guess that's that."

Billy's hand covered hers. "Do me a favor. Don't turn this one off until I come home. I want to know there's a light burning in our bedroom window for me."

She swallowed and nodded. "I won't turn it off."

He brought her hand up to his lips and kissed it, then he wrapped his fingers around hers. "You look tired."

"I am," she said, putting her arms around his waist. "It's been a long day." She followed up with a yawn. "Sorry."

"Go lie down. I'm gonna grab a quick shower."

Tilting her head back, she looked up at him. "Wake me if I fall asleep. This is your last night home for a few weeks. We've got business to attend to."

He held her a few seconds longer, running his hands through her hair and already missing the feel of it between his fingers.

"I'll be quick," he promised. And he was, but by the time he came back upstairs, Kate was asleep, her book open atop her chest. He marked her place, then set it on the nightstand and switched off the lamp. The only light in the room came from the electric candle in the window. As his eyes adjusted to the dark, he stood beside the bed and watched Kate sleep, feeling very much like the Grinch who stole Christmas.

Multicolored lights flickered through the amber liquid as Billy raised the glass to his lips. The whiskey rolled over his tongue, warm and oaky, burning just right as he swallowed. He lowered the glass and rested his head against the back of the chair.

The tree was smaller than he would have liked, but familiar, thanks to the ornaments he and Kate had collected since their first Christmas. The ornament Rhiannon had made in preschool, the one with her picture in the center surrounded by a frame of gilded macaroni, hung in a place of honor. Despite his melancholy, he smiled as he remembered the look of horror on her face that afternoon when they'd unwrapped it, and found half of the macaroni had been gnawed off by hungry mice. Kate had cleaned it and changed the ribbon hanger before she'd allowed Rhiannon to affix it to a branch.

Devin's handprint, memorialized in plaster the year he was born, hung near the top where it wouldn't get broken. Another ornament, Billy's favorite, was a framed picture of him and Kate, eight months pregnant with Rhiannon, her belly exposed, and him on his knees in front of her. Her hands resting on his head, she smiled down at him while he caressed the watermelon-sized bump as he pressed his lips above her navel.

From there his eyes traveled across the room to another photograph. Red, green, and yellow lights reflected on the glass, the only color on the black and white portrait hanging above the fireplace. Joey had taken it about six months after Devin was born, around the time Kate learned that her parents intended to sell her childhood home and move to Florida. While she never admitted it, probably not even to herself, he believed that subconsciously the picture was a "fuck you" to her mother. It was huge, maybe three foot by four foot. They were all naked, or at least it looked that way. Kate's hair covered her breasts and in her arms she held a pudgy Devin while Billy held Rhiannon. The portrait ended just above the scar from Kate's C-section and at a rather critical point for him, although the head of the viper tattooed just south of his lower abdominals was clearly visible. It was Kate's idea but Joey had orchestrated it, dubbing it "American Gothic Rocker."

Kate's mother had cringed the first time she'd seen it, which was also the last time. Evelyn had been to visit only once since she moved. Not that he missed her, but the old witch had two grandchildren who barely knew her.

Maybe that wasn't such a bad thing.

Thinking of Evelyn left a bitter taste in his mouth, which he tried to wash away with more whiskey. It also gave him an idea, one that Kate probably wouldn't go for, but it was worth a shot.

There was a soft rustling in the doorway.

"I thought you were going to wake me." Kate stood before him, wearing a football jersey from the University of Kansas that his cousin Robbie had sent him for Christmas a few years ago. Her legs and feet were bare, and her hair was messy and tangled. His cock twitched.

He set his empty glass on the coffee table and held out his arms. "C'mere."

Kate obeyed, climbing into his lap and tucking her head beneath his chin.

"I woke up and began to panic." Her voice was thick with sleep. "I thought it was the day after tomorrow and you were already gone."

Fuck. He hated this. He held her tightly with one arm, while his other hand traveled up her thigh, over her ass, and rested against her hip.

"Nah. You can't get rid of me that easily." Damn if his voice didn't catch. He gave himself a little time before he tried to speak again. "You know I don't want to go, right?"

He felt her nod.

"I've been thinking. I want you to hear me out before you answer." He gripped her shoulder. "Look at me." When he could see her eyes, he continued.

"I was thinking you should invite your mother to come for Christ—"

The way her body tensed you would have thought a snake had just slithered out from under the Christmas tree. He pressed his fingers to her lips. "I said hear me out." Her eyes flashed.

"If she's here, it will give you a bit of a break. You can finish your Christmas shopping and all that baking I'm sure you're still planning to do for half the damn town." Why she needed to bake dozens of cookies to drop off at the police and fire departments and for the rescue squad, he'd never understand. It's not like they'd ever had to call on any of them, but there was no arguing with her about some things.

"Plus, we have a private gig New Year's Eve in Manhattan. If your mother's here, you can meet me in the city. We'll spend the night, and come home together in the morning." He removed his fingers from her mouth. "Well? What do you think?"

"No."

Katie would usually do just about anything he asked of her, so her quick, negative response was surprising. Then again, it was her mother. He'd thought of asking their neighbor, Eileen, but Kate had said she and her husband, Marty, would be on a cruise over the holidays.

"That's one less day we're apart." His fingers snaked up her neck and into her hair. "And I don't want to start the New Year without you. Call me superstitious, but it kinda freaks me out."

"You're okay with spending Christmas without me but you can't manage New Year's Eve?"

"First of all, I'm not okay about Christmas. I don't have a fucking choice. I never thought that someday I'd be having second thoughts about doing something that I loved. I mean it. I've been sitting here, second-guessing all of it. You and the kids are what's important. I don't want to go, but if I don't, I'm out of the band. Maybe by the time this gig is over, I can give my own band another shot. But I can't be out of work for a month or two. My royalties won't keep us going that long."

She traced lazy circles over the tribal tattoo on his arm. "So how does my mother coming make any of that happen?"

"It doesn't. But it would allow you to be with me on New Year's Eve, and if that's all I get, then I want it."

Kate's sigh was a sure sign she was weakening. "What makes you think she'll come?"

Nothing made him think that. He just hoped, for once, Evelyn would do the right thing.

"Maybe just knowing I'm not here will do the trick," he said, teasing her. Uptight Evelyn was not a fan. Bad enough her daughter had run off with a tattooed, pierced, long-haired musician, she'd married him—five months pregnant and in a Methodist church. Maybe that was why she and Kate's father had put their house on the market and moved shortly after he and Kate had bought a house a few blocks away.

Nah. She was just an evil bitch who'd convinced her daughter to move back home so they could work on their relationship and so that the kids would have their grandparents, only to turn around and hurt her once again by leaving. At least Kate's father had come around soon after Rhiannon was born. Kate had taken it hard when he died of a massive coronary not long after he and her mother had moved to Boca.

But if Evelyn could make things a little easier on Kate while he was away, it would be worth it. He cupped her cheek. "Do it for me."

She let out a long, exhaustive breath. "Fine. But only because I don't want to start the year without you either." She wiggled around on his lap. "Now, I suggest we head upstairs and get busy. It's late."

He turned her until she was straddling him, then tugged her shirt over her head and grinned.

"Who says we have to go upstairs?"

CHAPTER 8

Kate didn't want to drive Billy's van into the city on New Year's Eve, so they agreed she would take the train from Dover, and he would drive himself to Newark Airport and park in long-term parking. Even if the rest of the band was flying into JFK or LaGuardia, he'd just fly to Newark and drive into the city. This way they could drive home together.

Not having to take him to the airport gave her plenty of time to work up the courage to call her mother. She'd seen her only three times since her father died. At the funeral, of course, and then once when she returned to Belleville when one of her friends won a prestigious teaching award. The last time had been a couple years earlier. Billy had a weeklong gig at a resort in Hilton Head, so they made a vacation out of it. On his day off, they had taken the hour-long drive to Savannah, where her mother had moved after her father's death.

The visit had been okay, but Kate had been glad it was only for an afternoon. She couldn't imagine spending a weekend with her mother, let alone an entire week. And now, here she was, calling to invite her to stay for three weeks.

She gripped the receiver in her hand. Three weeks was pushing it. Her mother would never agree to come for three weeks. Billy had deluded himself into thinking her mother would be helpful. Kate could do most of her baking and wrapping after the kids went to bed. Her mother could fly in the Tuesday before Christmas, and then leave the day after New Year's. Two weeks would be plenty. Kate pressed the numbers for the area code and stopped. Not surprisingly, she didn't know the number by heart. She dug around in the kitchen drawer for her address book.

She dialed the area code and the exchange before hanging up again.

What if her mother came and then decided two weeks was too long and wanted to leave before New Year's? It would defeat the whole purpose of her coming, because really, wasn't babysitting on New Year's Eve what was most important?

Yes. Two weeks was definitely too long. Christmas was on a Monday. If her mother flew in the Friday before, and then left the day after New Year's, that would be eleven days. Still a long time, but she would do her best to make it work.

This time when she dialed, she let it ring.

"Hi, Mom. It's me. Kate."

After a few beats of silence, her mother spoke. "Do you truly think it's necessary to identify yourself? I have one child, Kate. I presumed it was you when you said 'Hi, Mom.'"

Was it too late to hang up? Kate forged ahead. "I was calling to invite you to spend Christmas with me and the kids. Billy's on tour and won't be getting back to the East Coast until the end of December. So it'll just be us. Me, you, and the kids. They haven't seen you in such a long time, and they're really excited." That was a lie, of course. When Billy mentioned it that morning at breakfast, Rhiannon had reminded him, for the hundredth time, that she wanted an American Girl doll, while Devin had scrunched up his face and asked, "Who?"

"I know your husband likes flitting around the world, but why would he take a job that keeps him away from his family over the holidays? Are things that bad between the two of you?"

God, give me strength. "No, Mother. Things are not bad between us at all. The gig he was supposed to get fell through, and the band manager booked this. He really didn't have a choice in the matter."

"No, but you did. If you wanted to marry a tradesman, you know that Johnson boy was crazy about you." The only thing Kate's mother liked about Digger, aka "that Johnson boy"—who had been Kate's disaster of a prom date—was that he wasn't Billy. "At least he graduated from college." That was either a slam at Kate, who dropped out after one semester, or Billy, who dropped out at the beginning of his junior year—or both. "He has a degree in criminal justice now. I spoke with his mother recently. She told me he joined the Belleville Police Department. Did you know that? He might be chief someday."

If Kate's eyes rolled back any further she would see the inside of her skull.

"How wonderful for Digger. So about Christmas? Do you want to think about it and get back to me?"

"I don't know. I'd have to see if someone can water my plants and get my mail."

"You travel all the time, Mother. I'm sure there's someone you can ask." Kate pushed on. "I was thinking that maybe you could fly in the Friday before Christmas and stay until the Tuesday after New Year's. Billy will be flying into New York early New Year's Eve, and if you don't mind, I was hoping you'd watch the kids so that I can meet him in the city."

Silence.

More silence.

"Mom?"

"Is that what this is about? You need a babysitter?"

Yes. "No. Of course not. The kids and I will be alone, and I thought it would be a good chance for us to spend some time together. If you don't want to babysit, I can ask Eileen." *Who will be in the Caribbean, but you don't need to know that.*

"I guess it would be nice to see everyone again."

"Everyone?"

"Phyllis, Darlene, the Romanos."

And your grandchildren. Don't forget them.

"Oh! And I almost forgot!"

Thank you.

"The Romanos' Christmas party. If I come, I'll be able to go this year. You know your father and I never missed a single year until we moved."

How could she forget? It was the night of the Romanos' party that Kate had run off with Billy.

"So, is that a yes?"

"Yes, I think so. What a wonderful surprise!"

⁓

"What do you mean she's flying into Newark?" Joey asked. "Can't she program her broom to just land in your backyard?"

Kate stifled a laugh, unwilling to encourage him. "Apparently not. But at least she'll only be here for eleven days. Billy wanted me to have her come for three weeks. I whittled it down a bit."

"Whittled? Sounds like you hacked it in two."

Kate was already feeling guilty. Her mother had honestly sounded excited about coming. Over the past couple of days, Kate had begun preparing Rhiannon and Devin. She showed them pictures and told them about her mother and her father so that they would feel more comfortable when her mother arrived. Rhiannon had some vague recollection of her grandmother, or at least said she did, but Devin had begun to sound like an owl. Every time Kate mentioned her mother, he scrunched up his little face and responded with "Who?"

It seemed the concept of her being a mother and having a mother was too hard for him to grasp.

She pushed on with the real reason she was calling Joey. "I wanted to invite you to join us."

A loud clucking pierced her ear.

"Knock it off. Will you come for Christmas?"

This time he laughed.

"Joey. That's not a very gracious response to an invitation."

"I'm sorry. Were you serious?"

"Of course I'm serious. Why would I ask you if I didn't want you here? You know the kids want you here."

"I'm sure they do, but I think their mother just wants me to run interference. I've done that before. It doesn't work, and I don't feel like spending the holiday defending my sexuality to your mother, regardless of how much fun you must think it is for me."

He was right. Her mother had been horrible the last couple of times she'd seen him, but still. He was her best friend, and she wanted him there for Christmas.

"C'mon, please?" Begging wasn't beneath her.

"Sorry, doll. I already have plans. James and I have tickets for a matinee Christmas Eve and I'm having dinner with him and his family in Westport on Christmas Day. If I hadn't already accepted, I would come, you know that. For you, though. Not for your mother."

She sighed. "I know. It'll be fine. I'm just nervous, I guess."

"Don't be. You're an adult and she's a miserable old woman. Don't give her the power. If she starts being critical or hurtful, just put her in her place."

"Easy for you to say. You'll be eating pâté and drinking Dom Perignon. When are you leaving for Hawaii?"

"Day after Christmas. Two glorious weeks with nothing but sun, sand and sunscreen."

She couldn't remember ever being more jealous. "Sounds great."

"Don't get too excited."

"I'm sorry. Things just seem so weird right now. Billy won't be here for Christmas. My mother will. And then when I finally do get to see him, it won't be until New Year's Eve at some fancy party where I'll probably stand in the corner by myself all night, not knowing anyone there."

"What are you wearing?"

"I don't know. I can't think that far ahead. I have to see what's in my closet."

"Don't bother. There's nothing in your closet you can wear to a New Year's Eve party in Manhattan. Trust me."

"Then what do you suggest? I can't afford a fancy dress. It's Christmas, remember?"

"Um, hello. Fairy Godfather here. Let me find something for you."

"I can't ask you to do that."

He tsked loudly. "You didn't. Now if you're really good, Cinderella, maybe I'll turn your mother into a pumpkin."

CHAPTER 9

Pernicious Anemia had been on tour with Truth Monkey for less than a week, and Billy had yet to see Truth Monkey frontman Rafe Summerland sober. Like now, as he swayed over Billy, a bottle of Jack Daniels hovering over Billy's glass.

"I'm good," Billy said, covering his glass with his hand. The alcohol no doubt slowing Rafe's reflexes, several drops trickled from the bottle and onto Billy's knuckles. He yanked his hand away and scowled up at him.

"Sorry, man." Rafe tucked the opening of the bottle between his lips and threw his head back, draining the last of it.

The guy had to be a fucking pickle. Each morning, or whenever Rafe was awake enough to crawl out of his bunk, Billy watched him hover over a plate of sliced melon and scrambled eggs, a cigarette in one hand, and a screwdriver in the other. Not that Billy hadn't started his day a time or two with a little vodka to take the edge off, but every day? At this rate, Rafe's liver would look like a piece of beef jerky someday, if it didn't already.

Billy wiped his hand on the towel he'd had draped around his neck since the end of Pernicious Anemia's set. He wanted a shower and bed, but Rafe wanted to party, so instead of heading to the hotel where they'd be staying that night, the bus sat idling in the stadium parking lot.

A girl dropped down onto the leather sofa beside him. She had a wild mane of blonde hair and her glassy blue eyes were heavily lined with black. A hole was visible in her black textured stockings on the inside of her thigh, which he noticed when she crossed her legs. A tiny black leather skirt matched her boots. The neck of her sweater drooped over one shoulder, exposing a thin, black bra strap. They must all shop at the same store, he thought; Groupies R Us or something. He'd fucked hundreds of girls like her before he'd met Kate. They were practically interchangeable.

"He's hammered," she proclaimed, pointing at Rafe, as if he hadn't figured that out for himself.

"Belle," she said, holding out a hand with gnawed down fingernails and chipped black polish. When he didn't take it or answer, she pulled back. "That's okay, I know who you are." She gave a funny little laugh and leaned closer. Too close. Her perfume was so strong, it burned his throat. "Between me and you, I think you should be the headliner, but don't tell Rafe I said that."

"Yeah?" he asked. Of course he agreed with her.

Her eyes grew darker. "Oh, yeah," she whispered. "Without a doubt." The girl sitting next to her passed over a joint. The blonde shook her head and handed it to him. He took two deep hits, held his breath, and passed it back to her friend.

Belle shifted on the narrow sofa until her knee was pressing against his thigh.

"I saw you play before, you know. When you were with Viper. At the Re-Bar in Seattle." The pressure on his thigh increased. She leaned closer. "I'm pretty sure we hooked up."

He tipped his head back and emptied his glass. "I'm pretty sure we didn't."

Unfortunately, she didn't take it to mean he wouldn't. She just laughed and ran a hand over his thigh. "I guess we should do something about that then."

No fucking way. He stood. "Thanks anyway." He pushed past Belle and her friend, then squeezed around Kev Cunningham, Truth Monkey's lead guitarist, and Cam, the drummer for Pernicious Anemia, who were doing lines on the narrow table built against the wall of the bus.

"Where you going?" Cam called after him.

"Bed."

"Alone?" Kev asked with a laugh that Billy didn't appreciate. He usually kept to himself on tours. He didn't make friends easily, but he also didn't go out of his way to make enemies. This sonofabitch was asking for it though.

"Yeah, alone."

Rafe's legs were stretched across the opening between the lounge and the bunk area, blocking Billy's exit. Some tramped up little tart straddled him, shoving her cleavage into Rafe's eager face.

At this rate, they'd never get to the hotel.

Billy kicked Rafe in the shin. "Move," he demanded. When it seemed unlikely that would happen, he stepped over him, and into the bunk room, which was located between the two lounge areas. He hauled himself up into his bunk, stripped down to his boxers, and jammed in his ear plugs, determined to go to sleep. Being an inch taller than the mattress was long, he rolled onto his side and faced the wall with his knees bent. So much for sleeping in a real bed.

He'd just about fallen asleep when he felt the mattress dip.

Given his size and with another body in his bunk, it was nearly impossible to turn. The only thing he could do was twist his neck and peer over his shoulder.

"What the fuck?" he growled.

The girl from earlier, Belle, had climbed in beside him. And given the amount of skin touching his, he could only assume she'd lost her clothes between the lounge and his bunk.

If he turned, he'd be pressed up against her, and there wasn't enough clearance for him to sit up. "What the fuck?" he repeated, louder this time. He was straining his neck so hard it was beginning to cramp.

For a moment, the girl looked as if she might be second-guessing her decision to climb naked into his bunk, but it passed. Instead of leaving, she fucking smiled at him.

"Kev said you were tense, and I should help you relax." She stroked her fingers across his upper back. "I like your tattoos."

Kevin Cunningham was a dead man.

Billy tried to control his anger, store it up for the person who deserved it.

"Look, Belle, right?"

She nodded eagerly.

"I'm flattered, but I'm not interested." He pointed to the picture of Katie and his kids thumbtacked to the wall of his bunk. "I'm married. Happily. So if you don't mind—"

"Oh, I don't mind. I wouldn't go running back to your wife or anything." She produced a condom out of thin air and waved it at him. "I'm safe. Unless you just want a blow job. That's fine, too."

By sheer will, he practically bent himself in half and maneuvered himself to the end of the bunk. He swung out and dropped into the aisle. Rooting around in the sheets and trying not to disturb the part that was currently wrapped around the naked woman in his bed, he grabbed his jeans and slipped them on. He had no clue what had happened to his T-shirt, and at this point, he didn't care.

Belle leaned into the aisle. "Where're you going?"

"Away."

Billy grabbed his leather jacket from the empty bottom bunk and headed toward the front of the bus. He pushed through the second group of partiers and slid open the pocket door separating the driver from the living area.

Earl looked up from the driver's seat. A book was propped against the steering wheel. In his hand he held a hoagie, reeking of onions and dripping oil and vinegar onto the paper wrapper. Billy pulled the door closed and dropped into the captain's chair beside him.

"S'up?"

He slammed his head against the headrest. "How far is the hotel?"

"About two miles. You thinkin' about walkin'?"

"Actually, yeah."

Earl arched an eyebrow. "Like that? You ain't even wearing a shirt."

"I got a jacket. I just want to get to the hotel, take a shower, and sleep in a bed where I can straighten my legs and not run into anyone who doesn't belong there." He stared out across the nearly empty stadium parking lot. "How late does this usually go on?"

Earl slipped a parking stub into his book to mark his place. "With Rafe lately, it could go all night."

"Shit."

"If you really want to get out of here, I can call one of the crew to come pick you up."

"That would be fucking amazing, but I don't want to wake anyone."

Earl reached for the two-way radio on the dash and pointed it at Billy. "No problem. You're a good guy. You respect your wife and kids." He motioned behind him. "I don't see enough of that with this bunch."

Billy smiled at the "good guy" designation. A few years ago, he would have been partying just as hard. He just didn't see how any of it was worth losing what he had waiting for him at home. He'd never been homesick on a tour before. Hell. He'd never been homesick in his life. But this tour was different for some reason. He wasn't even enjoying himself on stage, and it was affecting his performance.

Earl radioed Carlos, the tour manager, who had just pulled out of the parking lot. He agreed to turn around and come back.

"Thanks, man." Billy slipped into his jacket. "You got a family, Earl?"

"A couple kids. They're grown. My wife and I split up when they were little. She couldn't handle me being on the road, and I couldn't handle staying in one place." He shrugged. "It is what it is."

A van pulled up next to the door. Billy rose and held out his hand.

"Thanks, buddy, I owe you."

"Nah, just keep your head on straight. You don't want to mess up a good thing."

Recalling how he'd already made one foolish mistake, Billy swallowed the lump that had formed in his throat. He gave Earl a nod and a pat on the shoulder and stepped off the bus.

It was after three by the time he'd showered and climbed into bed. As exhausted as he was, he couldn't sleep. It would be a shitty thing to wake Kate in the middle of the night, but in his heart and his gut, he knew she wouldn't mind.

The phone rang twice. When she answered, her voice was thick and heavy with sleep.

"Hey, babe." He spoke softly, as if that and not the jarring of the ringing phone might startle her.

He heard a low, familiar "Hmmm" before she answered. "Hey you."

"I'm sorry to wake you."

"S'okay. What time is it?"

The neon numbers on the alarm clock were the only light in his hotel room. "About twenty after three." He pulled the spare pillow across his chest. "I just needed to hear your voice."

"Where are you?"

Some of the tension from earlier began to dissipate. "A hotel outside Seattle." He stretched, relishing the feel of soft sheets and unencumbered space. "How're the kids?"

"Good," she murmured. "Excited about Santa. Your daughter wants to set a trap and catch him. She's under the impression that if she does, she gets an unlimited amount of toys."

"That's my girl."

Kate yawned. "She is indeed."

He should hang up, let her get back to sleep, but he wasn't ready to let her go yet.

"You all squared away with your mother?"

"Uh huh. She's coming on the twenty-second and staying until the second."

"I thought we agreed to have her come earlier so she could give you a hand."

"Nope. That was all you. Besides, without you here to run interference, this will be plenty. I'm getting stuff done after the kids go to bed." She yawned again. "I'm fine."

He felt like a jerk for waking her. "I'm sorry, babe. I can call you in the morning."

"No." It was almost like a moan. "Don't go." Judging by the grunt that followed, she must have sat up, maybe even turned on the light.

Well, if she was awake and willing to talk, he was game.

"What are you wearing?" he asked, using the lowest, sexiest voice he could manage.

She giggled. "Flannel pajamas, socks, one of your sweatshirts, and I haven't had a shower in two days."

"Oh, sexy." And it was. To him, everything about her was sexy.

CHAPTER 10

If Kate had a clue that she'd be a single parent throughout the month of December, she never would have volunteered to coordinate Santa's Workshop at the elementary school. For the last two months she'd poured over catalogs and ordered the inexpensive gifts the students would be able to buy for their parents and siblings during the two-day event. She'd spent the past week pricing and sorting items so that when they were unpacked at the school by her committee members, they could easily set them up in the designated areas. She'd even arranged for Santa to make an appearance so the little shoppers could tell him what they wanted for Christmas.

What she hadn't counted on, other than Billy being on the other side of the country, was that two-thirds of her committee would be struck down with the flu. Including Santa Claus.

After getting the news from "Mrs. Claus," Kate hung up the phone. She took several slow, deep breaths, and tried not to panic before giving herself a chance to think before she went spiraling off the deep end.

Marty!

With a renewed burst of energy, Kate grabbed the kids' jackets from the hooks by the back door and marched into the living room. She flicked off the TV.

"Here," she said to her stunned offspring. "Put on your coats."

"Why?" Rhiannon demanded. Devin stared at the blank TV screen, looking confused.

"We have to go out. Just for a few minutes. Come on." She picked up Devin's arm and slipped it into the sleeve of his jacket.

"I'm wearing my pajamas," he said mournfully.

"I know, buddy. We won't be too long. I need to go see Eileen and Marty."

"It's too cold to go out," Rhiannon whined. "Can't we stay here while you go?"

"You're six. What do you think? C'mon. Coats and boots. Let's go."

She should have warmed up the van, but considering they were going to drive all of thirty seconds, it seemed rather wasteful.

She pulled in behind Marty's Chrysler and opened the door.

"Let's go," she ordered, unbuckling Devin's seatbelt and expecting Rhiannon to take care of her own. She did not. Instead she melted into a tearful heap.

"I don't want to get out of the car! It's too cold."

"Rhiannon. It's cold in the car. Either way, you're going to be cold. I'm sorry. I know. I'm a mean Mommy, but I have no choice but to take you with me."

Her daughter's cries grew louder. She kicked the back of the seat. "I want my Daddy!"

One, two, three . . . Kate took a deep breath. "So do I, but he's not here. I'm doing the best I can." She hoisted Devin onto her hip. "Unbuckle your seat belt and get out of the car, now."

Rhiannon kicked the seat twice more, then moving as slow as was humanly possible, began to do as she was told.

"The longer you take, the longer we'll be out here in the cold. Do you want us all to get sick?" For the most fleeting of seconds the image of being curled up in bed with a hot cup of tea and a warm blanket, with nowhere to go and nothing to do, was vastly appealing. Unfortunately, she couldn't afford to get sick until Billy came home.

The back door opened. "What in Sam Hill is going on out there? Kate? What's wrong, honey?"

Kate trudged through the snow up Eileen's sidewalk.

"Nothing. I needed to talk to you. Here." She passed Devin to Eileen, then turned back toward the car. "If you know what's good for you, you'll get moving."

Kate rarely lost her temper with her children, but after the last two weeks, she was due. Rhiannon must have thought so, too, as she quickly jumped from the car and darted toward the house. Kate slid the door to the van closed and followed.

Inside, Rhiannon yanked off her mittens.

"Don't get undressed. We're not staying."

It was more than her daughter could bear. She collapsed into a heap on the kitchen floor. Kate took another deep breath and stared at the ceiling. This time she counted to ten.

"Rhiannon, sweetheart," Eileen said. "Take your brother into the living room and say hi to Marty. I'll bring you each a cookie. Okay?"

With a smug look at her mother, Rhiannon tugged off her hat and took her brother by the hand. Static electricity made a spikey golden halo around her stubborn little head.

"Thank you," Kate said when the kids had disappeared into the other room, "but we really can't stay. I just needed to talk to you, and I thought it would be harder for you to say no if you saw how pathetic I looked."

Eileen guided her to a chair at the kitchen table, and then snatched the kettle from the stove and began to fill it.

"Nonsense," she insisted when Kate said again that they couldn't stay. "Tea is good for whatever ails you. And you look like you could use at least two cups."

While they waited for the water to boil, Kate filled Eileen in on her mother's planned visit.

"So Evelyn is actually coming for Christmas." She clucked several times. "It's about time."

Kate played with the fringes on the placemat in front of her. "Well, to be fair. I haven't really invited her before. But I am surprised she's coming. Maybe she's mellowing a bit, or maybe she just wants to see her grandchildren."

The water boiled and Eileen filled three mugs. She set one before Kate. The second she carried into the living room for Marty, along with two store-bought oatmeal cookies for Rhiannon and Devin. When she returned, she placed a few more cookies on a plate, set it on the table, and then sat down across from Kate.

"They're watching Rudolph," she explained. "Devin is sitting in Marty's lap, and Rhiannon is curled up beside him."

It wouldn't be the first time her children had climbed all over Marty or Eileen like they owned them. These were the grandparents she would have wished for her children if she'd had a choice. Despite all the deep breaths she'd been taking over the past few days, she finally felt like she could exhale.

"Thank you."

Eileen stirred some artificial sweetener into her tea and took a sip. "So why did I need to see how pathetic you looked?"

Kate dunked a cookie into her tea.

"The Santa's workshop at the elementary school is tomorrow and almost all of my committee has the flu, including Santa. I was hoping—scratch that. I'm begging you to come help me tomorrow and Thursday. And I'm not above begging Marty to play Santa."

Kate shoved the entire cookie in her mouth. "Pweese."

Eileen snickered. "You know I taught seventh and eighth grade because I have no patience for grade schoolers, right?" Kate nodded. "And I'm older and crankier now than I was when I taught school, right?" She nodded again. Eileen took a deep breath. "But for you, I guess I can make an exception. What do you need me to do?"

Kate swallowed. "Everything."

Eileen blinked.

"I'm serious. It will be me, you and two other mothers, if they don't also come down with this mysterious flu." She took a too-quick sip of her tea and burned her tongue. "I'm feeling less than charitable, but I'm beginning to wonder if some of them aren't sick at all, just too busy to help out. I had plenty of volunteers back in September. Suddenly, they're dropping like flies."

"Eh, it wouldn't be the first time. They're like people on committees everywhere. They just don't want to work."

Kate felt guilty even suggesting it, but the stress of the holiday had stripped her of her holiday spirit. "And Marty? I know he has a Santa suit. I was hoping he'd come over for a few hours on Thursday. Just the one day. The principal told me how excited the kids have been to have Santa at school. This is my first year doing anything like this, and I don't want to fail right out of the gate."

Eileen reached across the table and clasped Kate's hand in her own. "You could never be a failure. Kate, darling, you have so much heart and spirit, and you always try to do the right thing. No one would fault you even if you called the whole thing off."

Kate's heart sank. Was this Eileen's way of telling her she wouldn't help?

"I can't call it off! I remember being a little kid and being so excited to be able to buy a present for my mother and father with my own money." There was both joy and pain threaded through the memory. Hot tears pricked the backs of her eyes. "I understand if you can't help. I'll manage somehow, but I can't cancel."

"Oh, sweetie, no. I'm not telling you to cancel. I'll help you, and I'm sure Marty will too."

The tears spilled over anyway, but these were from relief.

Finally. Something was going her way.

CHAPTER 11

The phone rang at least a dozen times before Billy finally hung up. It would be after eight back home. The kids were usually in bed by now. The only thing he could imagine was that Kate was out shopping. The image of her dragging the kids around past their bedtimes, trying to do everything by herself, made him feel worse than he already did. And that was saying something.

Cam thumped him on the shoulder. "C'mon, man. We got soundcheck."

"Now?"

"Yeah, Rafe's still too hungover to get off the bus, so Carlos says we gotta go first."

"Where are the rest of the guys?"

"They're plugging in. Carlos sent me to find you."

Depending on how long soundcheck took, he might not get another chance to call Kate that night. She'd sounded so run down the last time he spoke with her, it would be cruel to call her late again, wake her up, even though it would gnaw at him wondering why she wasn't home.

Damn. He'd never been like this before. First chance he got, he was buying a mobile phone. This way he could call Kate whenever he wanted, and she could reach him instead of having to wait for him to call her. He didn't care what the damn things cost.

With his mind 2,800 miles away, he rounded a corner and slammed into Kev and some chick.

Billy reached out to steady the woman he'd nearly bowled over. "Whoa! Sorry," he said, directing his comments at her. As for Kevin, he would like nothing more than to see his ass sprawled out on the ground. The guy was a first-class asshole.

"Watch it, rock star!" the sonofabitch snarled.

Chances were looking pretty good that before this tour was over, Billy's fist would be connecting with Kev's mouth. For now, he just glared at him. "I said I was sorry."

"What's your hurry?"

"I've got soundcheck." Billy stepped to the side to pass him, but Kevin moved in the same direction, blocking him. Not only was he an asshole, he was a dumb asshole.

"Did you know my man here makes children's records?" Kev said to the girl attached to his side. "They actually gave him a Grammy for it."

The girl blew a large pink bubble and bit down, making a loud pop. "That's nice." She drew the huge wad of gum back into her mouth.

"Fuck that!" Kev snarled. "Want to know how many Grammy's I got, rock star? Six. Real ones. Not some fucking kid shit."

Billy tried to ignore the familiar itch in his palms, and instead of curling his hands into fists, he flattened them against his thighs. One punch and he'd lay this sucker out. Only then he'd find himself on the next plane back to New Jersey. Was that what he wanted?

Actually, it was, but he needed to reel it in because he couldn't afford to let his temper get the best of him.

"What's your problem, Kev, huh? You've had a hard-on for me since I got on this tour."

"Yeah, right. A hard-on. Ha!" Kevin grabbed his little friend's ass. "You're the only one who gives me a hard-on, babe."

If he wasn't so pissed, Billy would have laughed. Instead, he glared at the guitarist. "I asked you what your problem was. I don't bother you. Why don't you just leave me the fuck alone?"

Kev's stance was one that said he wasn't afraid to go a few rounds with Billy. The damn fool even took another step closer.

"I'll tell you what my problem is." Kevin drilled a finger into Billy's chest. "I'm sick of your attitude. You've got the chance of a lifetime, opening for Truth Monkey, and you're moping around like you're doing us all a big fucking favor being here. If I was Rafe, I'd send your ass home and get someone on this tour who actually wants to be here. That's what's pissing me off. Now get the fuck out of my way."

He drove his shoulder into Billy's and pushed past him, dragging the chick behind him.

"Bye, Billy," she called over her shoulder like they'd all just exchanged pleasantries.

For as much as he wanted to send Kev somewhere into next week, the fucker wasn't too far off. Yeah, he knew he could be difficult and moody. Dangerous even. But mopey? *I'll show him mopey.* He should've slugged the bastard when he had the chance.

Instead, Billy jammed his hands in his pocket and headed backstage.

CHAPTER 12

Despite the record number of parents stricken with sudden flu-like symptoms, most of Belleville's children appeared to be in robust health and able to attend school the week before Christmas and as such, had flocked to Santa's Workshop.

It was a regular Christmas miracle, Kate thought, with much less generosity than was typical for her, especially since she was convinced most of her committee—stressed out parents like herself—had more important Christmas-related things to do and had bailed on her. At least she'd had Marty and Eileen, who were now gathered around their kitchen table with her and her children, polishing off the last of the pizzas she had purchased as a small thank you. Pizza was the least she could do after they came to her rescue. Eileen had dug in her heels and worked side by side with Kate both days. And Marty? He'd been the perfect Santa. And why not? The man owned his own Santa suit.

"I can't thank you two enough," Kate said after dinner, crumpling her paper plate and tossing it into the trash. "I wouldn't have made it through the last two days without you. Even if Billy had been home, I'd have never talked him into working at the school for an hour, let alone two days. He loves his kids. But other people's? Not so much."

Rhiannon's chair scraped across the kitchen floor. "Can I watch TV?"

"No, sweetie. We need to go home. You and Devin need a bath and you have school tomorrow, and then we're driving to the airport to pick up your grandmother."

"Who?" Devin asked, looking up from the bits of cheese he'd been picking off of his pizza.

Eileen snorted softly. "Do you want me to keep them while you go to the airport?"

"Don't you have to get ready for your trip?" Kate forced a smile. "And besides, who'll keep my mother entertained on the ride home if the kids don't go?"

"I'm guessing that would be you, but I get your point. And to be honest, I do have laundry and packing. We're leaving for the airport right after church Christmas morning."

"I can't believe you're flying on Christmas."

"We got a great discount for flying that day. Besides, we'll be having Christmas dinner in the Caribbean. Not a bad trade off."

Joey was going to Hawaii. Eileen and Marty to the Caribbean. Billy would be in Los Angeles. Kate and her children would be celebrating with her mother.

The already tense knot between her shoulders grew tighter.

"You okay?" Eileen asked.

Other than feeling sorry for herself, Kate was fine. And she certainly wasn't going to start whining after Eileen and Marty had busted their asses to save hers.

"I'm just tired. Once I get the kids off to bed I have to finish my baking and make up the trays to deliver in the morning. I also need to finish up the list of things I still need to pick up. I'm hoping to stop on my way back from the airport and get that out of the way. The last thing I want to do is make a trip to the mall three days before Christmas, but I don't really have much choice."

She wiped Devin's hands, and then helped him into his jacket while Eileen snugged Rhiannon's hat over her head.

"I'll give you a call tomorrow night. Marty and I will pop over to say hello to Evelyn. Will that be okay?"

"I'm pretty sure she's going to the Romanos' party tomorrow night. How about Saturday? Come for dinner. I owe you something much more substantial than pizza."

"Saturday's fine, but just drinks. I know how you like to fuss, and you're running ragged as it is. We'll pop over for a little drinky-poo, say hello, and be on our way." When Kate attempted to argue, Eileen raised her hand. "Nothing doin.' One drink. But as for the Romanos, they're not having a party this year. Tony just had a hip replacement, and I heard Anna decided to skip it this year. Can't say that I blame her."

Kate hadn't heard about Mr. Romano. Her mother would have known, of course, although she hadn't mentioned it. "That's too bad. I honestly think that party was the reason my mother agreed to come." She gave Eileen a kiss on the cheek and tugged on her mittens. "Do you want to make it Friday then?"

"Heavens, no!" She lowered her voice and winked. "Let's give the Dragon Lady a good night's rest before she has to make nice."

Kate rushed the kids through their bath. Read them each a story, and then tucked them in with lights out just after eight. She pulled her cookie dough from the refrigerator, turned the oven on to preheat, and set out her cookie sheets and rolling pin. She was dragging, so she put on the kettle, hoping that a cup of tea would give her the boost of energy she needed to finish off the last two batches of cookies.

While she waited for the water to boil, she checked the messages on the answering machine. The first was from Billy.

"Hey, babe. I'm sorry I missed you again." He let out a deep breath. "I really fucking miss you. This sucks. I'm not sure when I can get to a phone again. We're heading out right after the show and driving through the night to be in Sacramento by morning. You're probably exhausted, so I'm not going to call and wake you later. I'll call you as soon as we get to the hotel. Kiss the kids for me and tell them how much I miss them." There was a long silence. "I love you, baby."

Kate slumped against the counter. He sounded awful. It didn't help they'd missed so many conversations. What she wouldn't give to be able to call him back.

The kettle whistled. Kate filled her mug, added some honey, and played the second message.

"Hello, Kate. It's mother. I'm afraid there's been a change of plans. I'm not going to be able to make it after all. Something's come up, and I've had to cancel my trip. I hope you'll understand. Give my best to the children. You can have them call me Christmas afternoon to thank me for their presents. I should be home until two. Take care, darling."

Kate dropped onto the stool beside her and stared at the answering machine. Stunned didn't quite cover what she was feeling, and she didn't know whether to laugh or cry.

So she did both.

CHAPTER 13

Rage might be the best way to describe Billy's emotion when he called the next morning and Kate told him about her mother's cancelled trip.

"What the fuck does that mean, 'Something's come up?'"

"I don't know. She didn't elaborate, and I didn't bother to call her back. What's the point? To be honest, I'm almost not surprised."

"Sonofabitch." He'd said it low and grumbling, but she heard him nonetheless.

"The worst of it is, I'm not going to be able to come to New York for New Year's Eve now."

There was a loud crash on Billy's end. Something had probably just gone flying.

"Babe, I'm sorry," she said, softening her voice, trying to soothe him from two thousand miles away. "I don't know how to fix this."

"It's not your fault," he growled into the phone, "and I'm not mad at you. But I could choke your mother. We should've known better than to count on her."

Having been about to walk out the door when Billy called, Kate unbuttoned her coat and tugged off her hat. "I know. I wish I could think of something else. If it wasn't overnight, I'd get a babysitter, but with Marty and Eileen away, there just isn't anyone else I trust with the kids, other than Joey, of course, but he's leaving for Hawaii on Wednesday."

Billy was so quiet that if Kate hadn't heard noise in the background, she would have thought they'd been disconnected.

"Babe, listen to me."

He let out a long, low sigh. "I'm here."

"I'm worried about you. You're taking this whole thing really hard, and you shouldn't be. You're working. You're supporting your family. I miss you, but I understand, and I don't resent what you're doing. We'll celebrate when you come home." She struggled to find the right things to say. If she could just make him laugh, that might help. "It's just a day. You know me. I'm late for everything. So we have Christmas a week late. Big deal, right? We'll do the whole thing as a family, from reindeer-shaped pancakes to forgetting the chestnuts in the oven and burning them. And I'll do something special with the kids to celebrate Christmas Day too, so they won't be missing out on anything. We'll do it all, and it'll be great. You'll see."

He didn't answer.

"Are you there?"

"Yeah."

She closed her eyes and pictured him. It was like she had some special powers that enabled her to see him on the other side of the country. He was at a payphone, his head bent, probably even pressed against the wall, and she saw his arm draped over the phone. His hair was in a ponytail, and since he was still in northern California, he was most likely wearing his leather jacket. The image was so vivid, she had to know if she was right.

"What are you wearing?"

Billy laughed and some of the tension leeched from his voice. "C'mon, babe," he cooed. "I want nothing more than to play that game with you, but I might get arrested since I'm standing in a public corridor."

Finally. It felt good to hear him laugh. "Sorry to disappoint you, but I wasn't trying to get you hot and bothered. I was just trying to picture you right now. Although, I wouldn't mind some alone time with you, even if it was just over the phone."

"Me too. God I miss you."

"Ditto." She slumped against the counter. "Just remember what I said: This is your job. Do it well. Enjoy yourself when you can. And know we're all fine and that we miss you and we love you."

"I love you, too. Kiss my babies."

"Definitely."

With that, they hung up. Kate needed to get moving if she was going to deliver all of her cookie trays and get to the grocery store before she needed to pick up Devin from preschool, but knowing how depressed Billy was about this tour was weighing on her. She thought about what she'd said to him about somehow having two Christmases. She needed to make it happen.

She pulled out her notepad and started making a list. For starters, she'd hold back some of the kids' gifts, and then rewrap the rest of them after Christmas so they could unwrap them again with him on New Year's Day. Billy would love that, and so would the kids. And instead of making her traditional Christmas dinner, she'd save that for the following week when he was home. On Christmas Day she'd make the kids' favorites. Macaroni and cheese. Chicken fingers. Hot dogs. There wouldn't be a green vegetable in sight. She jotted down everything she'd need from the store.

About halfway through her list, she felt lighter. She was no longer upset that her mother wasn't coming. She'd make a special Christmas for her children, and then a week later, when Billy was home, they'd do it all again as a family.

Two Christmases. It would be perfect—or as close to perfect as she could make it.

CHAPTER 14

Early afternoon and SuperFresh was packed. With Christmas just a couple of days away, Kate wasn't the only one trying to finish up their grocery shopping. She navigated her cart down the aisle, checking things off her list. She had everything she needed except for cheese, cream, and milk. She was wondering if she needed anything else for the kids' stockings, when she rounded the corner and drove her cart straight into the back of a police officer.

"Oh my God!" Horrified, she stepped back and slammed into a woman reading the label on a box of elbow macaroni, knocking it out of her hand. Kate dove to pick it up, not realizing the shopper was doing the same thing until their two heads banged together. Staggering slightly, Kate mumbled an apology while the woman yanked the box out of her hands and stalked down the aisle, presumably getting as far away from her as possible.

Gripping the handle of her cart, Kate turned back to the officer and gulped.

"Digger! Jeez. Imagine running into you here. I mean . . . um . . . Well, of course I didn't mean to actually *run* into you. That was totally an accident." She waved her list in front of him. "I was looking at my list. Checking it twice, ya know?" She laughed, but whatever the sound was that had erupted from her mouth had seemed somewhat maniacal.

Of all people to run into—literally or figuratively.

Despite moving back to Belleville four years earlier, Kate hadn't seen Digger once, which was fine by her. He'd gone off to college or the police academy or something. But hadn't her mother said something about him being back in Belleville? Swell. Last time she'd seen Digger she and Billy were having sex in Billy's van behind the high school. Real sex—like Billy was actually *inside* her when Digger rapped on the window and ordered them out of the van. Acting completely out of character, Kate had immediately told him to fuck off and threatened to call his mother. Good move. Hopefully there was some kind of statute of limitations on having sex in a public parking lot.

Judging by the heat radiating off her cheeks, they must be crimson about now.

Digger looked a little unnerved himself. He cleared his throat and gave her an uneasy smile.

"Hi, Kate. How're you doing?"

Not quite as tall as Billy, Digger was no longer the skinny boy he'd been in high school. Even through his police issue jacket and uniform, she could see that he'd bulked up considerably. His dark hair was still cut short, but no longer in the flattop that he'd always worn. And other than that first, brief moment of uneasiness, he exuded a sense of confidence and authority. It was an attractive look on him—not that he needed any help in that department. He was a good-looking guy; he always had been. But no matter how relentlessly he'd pursued Kate in high school, she'd just never been interested. She'd accepted his invitation to prom because like all the girls in her class, she'd wanted to go. And she thought he understood they were going as friends.

Unfortunately, he hadn't gotten that memo. The night had ended in disaster, with groping on his part and tears on hers. He'd tried several times to apologize, but Kate wasn't having it. She'd finally given him the opportunity right before she left for college, where she'd met Billy a couple of months later.

But that was old news, right? Water under the bridge and all that. Still. She couldn't shake the feeling of self-consciousness about her parking lot exploits.

"So I guess congratulations are in order. And welcome back, too."

His eyebrows dipped. "Congratulations?"

"You know, for your job and all."

"Oh." The frown lines eased. "I've been back since October. My dad was retiring, so I not only filled the opening with the police force, I bought my parents' house when they moved to Florida." He tapped the badge on his chest. "I'm a sergeant now."

"Oh, October. And wow, your parents' house. Good for you. I love Victorian architecture. Nice. I guess I don't get out much. Or arrested." This time when she laughed it sounded like someone was strangling a donkey. Why couldn't she have run into him when she had the kids with her? One of them would have had to go to the bathroom or something by now.

"So, you have kids, huh?"

Was he a mind reader as well as a cop? She tucked a strand of hair behind her ear. Digger's eyes followed her hand and lingered on her wedding ring. She shifted nervously from one foot to the other, unsure how to answer such a simple question.

"Kids." He pointed to her cart. "It looks like you have kids."

Cocoa Puffs, Lucky Charms, hotdogs, marshmallows, cocoa mix, two small boxes of crayons, and three boxes of Kraft Macaroni and Cheese—even though she'd planned to make her own from scratch, she was buying the boxed kind for insurance—some chicken strips, and two cans of pork 'n beans. She had kids all right.

She nodded. "Two. This is for our Christmas dinner."

"Oh." His eyes swept the cart again and the frown lines returned. "I see."

Doubtful, but she didn't feel like explaining. She pointed to the two Hungry Man dinners he held in his hands, and for a moment, she felt sorry for him. Going home to that huge house by himself, eating a TV dinner.

"I'm guessing no kids for you yet, huh?"

He looked down and shrugged. "No kids. No wife. No girlfriend." When he looked up again, he smiled sheepishly. "Can't cook either."

"There's nothing to it. Honestly. I love to cook. Do it every day." She waved her hand over her cart, and her smile came more naturally this time. "Don't let this fool you. I really am a good cook."

"You better not be misrepresenting yourself to an officer of the law."

She laughed. "Cross my heart and hope to die." An idea began to formulate. She had a few single girlfriends. If she could fix Digger up with one of them, maybe she wouldn't feel so bad about hurting his feelings back in high school. "In fact, you'll have to come for dinner some night. We'll make it a party or something. What do you think?"

He looked like he was trying to decide if she were telling the truth.

"You mean it? I figured after the last time I saw you—"

Was it too much to hope he would have forgotten that? "Please! Let's not mention that again. Ever." She covered her face with her hands until she heard him laugh.

"You got it. Consider it forgotten." When she took away her hands he was beaming down at her. "And yes. I'd love to come for dinner. I haven't had a good home-cooked meal since my mother packed her pots and pans and headed south."

"Wonderful!" She was already scanning her mental list of available friends. Toni had broken up with her most recent boyfriend, but she just couldn't picture the two of them together. Toni had earned a doctorate, and although she was an archeologist, Kate couldn't picture her dating someone whose nickname was "Digger," no matter how ironic it would be. Besides, they were on opposite ends of the intellectual spectrum. Her friend Pam might be perfect. A kindergarten teacher and a cop? They were made for each other. That was easy.

"It was really nice seeing you again, Digger. I'm sure we'll run into each other again soon. Hopefully I won't be doing something illegal." She laughed. "Either way, I'll definitely be in touch."

She swung the cart into the aisle and pushed past him. "Take care. Merry Christmas."

As she hurried toward the dairy case to collect the last few items on her list, she thought about how surprising it was that she hadn't tried matchmaking before, especially since it seemed she might have a knack for it.

The hardest part, as far as she could tell, would be getting Billy on board.

CHAPTER 15

Billy didn't want to be seen as mopey, nor did he want to get drunk and party like just about everyone else on the tour just to prove that he wasn't, so he kept to himself more than usual.

He felt a little better after talking with Kate that morning, but it still didn't take away the sting of missing Christmas with her and the kids. She would make sure the kids had a good Christmas, and she'd do it all over again for him, despite all the work involved. So no matter how fucking depressed he was, the next time they talked he'd make damn sure he sounded upbeat, as if none of this bothered him and he wasn't counting the days until January 1.

But that was exactly what he was doing—counting the days.

With the applause still ringing in his ears, he loped down the steps at the back of the stage and handed his Strat off to one of the roadies, then hit the shower in the dressing room. Rafe had been drinking most of the afternoon, and while chances were good he might pass out as soon as the show was over, he might also sober up enough to want to party afterward. The bus would be pulling out and heading for LA that night, but that wouldn't slow Rafe down. Billy had woken up too many mornings to find strange chicks sitting at the little table in the kitchenette, nursing hangovers on either side of the Truth Monkey frontman before getting a one-way ticket back home from Carlos.

Billy's only hope of getting some sleep was if he could get back to the bus before everyone else. Hopefully, he'd sleep through the night and wake up one day closer to getting home.

The bus was empty when he climbed aboard. No one to talk to or explain why he was turning in so early. He hoisted himself into his bunk and pulled the picture of Katie and the kids off his wall. He took it last Christmas. The three of them were wearing matching pajamas. Kate sat cross-legged in front of the tree with Devin in her lap. Rhiannon was curled up beside her, her curly blonde hair braided into one long strand over her shoulder, just like her mother's.

He couldn't believe it was possible, but knowing there would be no picture of the three of them Christmas morning was making him feel even worse.

He planted three soft kisses on the photograph, then tacked it back onto the wall, close to his head. He slipped in his ear plugs, rolled onto his side, facing the picture, and hoped he'd dream of home.

Kate coughed and pressed her naked body against his back, her arm snugged around his waist. It seemed like forever since he'd felt her touch. Pushing back, he shimmied his ass against her, and covered her arm with his own, weaving his fingers between hers. The bed rocked gently, the hum of the tires against the road a steady lullaby.

Billy blinked, struggling to get his bearings. He was definitely on the bus, which meant whoever was curled up against him was not his wife.

"Sonofabitch!" He pushed the arm off him and reaching up behind him, turned on the light. The girl beside him squinted and pushed up onto her elbow.

"Hey," she said in a voice thick with sleep.

"Who the fuck are you?" he demanded. "And what the fuck are you doing in my bunk?"

She yawned loudly, giving him a view of her dental work and a whiff of .whatever she'd been drinking that evening.

"Kev said—"

He didn't wait for her to finish. It wasn't easy, but he climbed over her and jumped out of the bunk, then stalked all of three steps to Kev's bunk. He tore open the curtain, and before the sonofabitch knew what was happening, Billy yanked him out of a deep sleep and onto the floor. Which he hit. Hard.

"What the fuck?" Kev snarled, trying to sit up.

"I don't think so, fucker." Billy pushed him down with the bottom of his foot, pinning him in place. "You told her to get into my bunk? Is there something wrong with you?" Raising his foot off Kevin's chest, Billy spun around and reached past the stunned woman cowering in his bunk and tore the picture of his family off the wall. By now, all of the curtains had been pulled open, except for Rafe's. Kevin struggled to get up. This time Billy let him, before pushing him up against the wall, his forearm under Kevin's throat.

"You see this?" He shoved the picture in Kev's face.

"This is my wife, Katie, and my kids. My six-year-old, Rhiannon, and my four-year-old, Devin. I love my fucking wife, and I don't cheat on her. If that's the way you want to live your life, that's your problem, but keep your whores and your groupies the fuck away from me. I don't fool around. You got it?"

When he let go, Kev slid against the wall, until he could get his footing. And then the fucker spoke.

"That's not what I heard."

Billy's right fist connected with Kev's jaw, snapping his head back and making a sickening thud against the thin laminate wall.

"That's for my wife."

His left fist rose up from his hip and landed square in Kev's gut. The bastard doubled over onto the floor as Cam jumped into the fray and pushed Billy back against the bunks. "Stop! He's not worth it. Just walk away. Cool the fuck down."

Billy leaned around Cam, his finger stabbing the air in Kev's direction. "That last one was for my kids. You pull shit like that on me again, and you won't stand up for a long time. Trust me."

He reached around the woman in his bed and grabbed his pillow and blanket.

"I'll go," she said, tearfully, clasping the sheet around her.

"I don't give a fuck what you do."

With all the commotion, Billy hadn't noticed that the bus had stopped moving. As he stalked into the lounge toward the front, he saw Earl standing in the door to the cockpit. Billy slammed the pocket door shut.

He glared at Earl. "I'm sorry, but I've had it with his bullshit."

Earl shrugged, but when he lifted his hand, he gave Billy a thumb's up. "Hey," he said. "Not my problem, right?"

Billy dropped his pillow onto the leather sofa, and himself beside it.

"Nope. I guess it isn't."

CHAPTER 16

Kate had barely said "hello" before Joey began regaling her with the wonders of the dress he'd found for her to wear on New Year's Eve.

"It's perfect! You're gonna hate it at first, but hear me out."

That sounded promising; not that it mattered anymore.

"Joey—"

"Hush. Now listen. It's made of this shimmery gold fabric with a draped neckline that falls off the shoulders. And it's short. I mean really short, but with your legs? Mwa!" She heard a kissing sound and pictured him with puckered lips and his fingers up to his mouth, like the guy on the pizza boxes. "It's gorgeous, and you, my dear, will be irresistible. Not that you weren't irresistible before, but the eunuch might need more encouragement since his little alteration."

She lowered the heat under her cheese sauce. "What the hell are you talking about?"

"The eunuch. The rock star, remember? Snip snip? Ringing any bells?"

"Oh for—He had a vasectomy, Joey. He wasn't castrated!"

"Potayto-potahto."

"Hardly. Trust me. He doesn't need any enticement to lure him into my bed. In fact—"

"Stop! You're making my ears bleed."

"You started it." She wedged the phone between her ear and her shoulder so she could drain the cooked macaroni into a colander.

He pushed on. "Anyway, the dress is a-maz-ing. I can either send it to you and you should have it by the beginning of next week, or I can leave it at my apartment and you can just get ready here. As a matter of fact, if you and the rock star want to stay here instead of a hotel, you're welcome to."

Although she and Billy wouldn't be spending New Year's Eve together now, she couldn't help but laugh at Joey's offer. "So you're saying you wouldn't mind Billy in your bed."

"Let's not go there," he answered flatly.

"I didn't think so. Thank you, for everything, but it's no longer necessary. My mother's not coming, so not only will the kids and I be alone for Christmas, I'll be ringing in the new year by myself."

"Are you kidding me? What the hell happened? I thought she was already there, haunting the old neighborhood."

"I notice you didn't even ask about her."

"Because I don't give a shit. Sorry, but that's the truth."

Kate sighed. Could she blame him?

"Why'd she cancel?

"I have no idea. She left a message on the answering machine saying something came up and that the kids could call her on Christmas Day, which means not to call her before. Maybe she never planned to come at all. Honestly, she seemed more excited about being able to go to the Romanos' Christmas party than she did about seeing us. Eileen told me Mr. Romano just had surgery, so there's no party. Maybe that's why she decided not to come. I have no clue, and at this point, I'm not sure I care."

Joey was quiet for a moment, and when he spoke, there was a different quality to his voice. It was softer, gentler. "You do care. I wish you didn't, but I know you're hurting. Let it go, Kate. Focus on the people who love you and let that shit go. It'll do nothing but eat you up inside if you let it."

Her chest felt tight and her eyes burned. She refused to cry. Not about her mother. Not anymore. She swallowed down her feelings.

"I'm fine. I'm disappointed about not being able to spend New Year's Eve with Billy, but I should've known better than to depend on my mother."

To stop herself from getting emotional, she veered the conversation toward her Christmas Day plans for a kids' feast and how she was going to recreate Christmas for Billy a week later.

"I'm jealous. I love your mac and cheese."

She laughed. "Like you'd eat all those carbs."

"For your mac and cheese, I would drown in carbs—drenched in cheese sauce." He was teasing, of course, but a moment later, he grew serious. "Now I feel even worse about going away."

"Don't. I told you, we're fine. Just promise me you'll visit when you get back from Hawaii. Bring me a coconut. Or a pineapple."

"How about a grass skirt."

"Even better."

CHAPTER 17

Concerts in LA always brought the energy, and this one was no different. It was welcome, too. Billy had moved through the past few weeks like he'd been phoning it in. Sleepwalking. That wasn't typical for him, not when it came to his music, but with things weighing so heavily on his mind, he just couldn't seem to shake himself from the funk.

But tonight was different. Pernicious Anemia rocked the opener and the crowd's response reminded him of why he did what he did. And to top it off, while he'd half expected to get fired for the fight with Kev, it seemed Rafe, in a moment of sobriety, had lit into his lead guitarist and told him to back the fuck off. At least he didn't have that asshole to worry about for now.

Still riding a high after their set, Billy grabbed a quick shower, and then joined Cam and the rest of the band to watch Truth Monkey from backstage.

He had to give Rafe credit. Despite the Jack Daniels and whatever else was pumping through his veins—he gave one hell of a performance. And he was in rare form tonight. The entire set was well-orchestrated, from the blinding light show to the roadie, who under the cover of darkness, slipped onto the stage to replace Rafe's empty bottle of JD.

Billy signaled as he exited the stage. "You got any of that to spare?"

Cam raised his nearly empty bottle of Bud in support of Billy's proposal.

With a thumb's up, the roadie jogged off and returned with two bottles of JD.

"Rafe's private stock," he said. "Merry Christmas." Then he slunk back to the wings to await his next order. What a life. The same shitty schedule as the band, but none of the glory. Some of these guys, especially the techs, were excellent musicians who just hadn't caught a break. Yet they lived to run and fetch and tune someone else's guitar in the dark. God bless 'em.

The arena erupted with the final notes of Truth Monkey's encore. Billy grabbed one of the bottles of Jack and left the other with Cam and the boys. "I'm claiming this baby as my own. See you guys on the bus."

With a benefit concert scheduled for early the next afternoon, Billy was glad Carlos had booked them into a hotel in Hollywood that night. He was aching to sleep in a real bed. He just hoped that Rafe would be willing to hold off his afterparty until they reached the hotel. If not, Billy had already left word with one of the guitar techs to come find him before they headed out.

Alone on the bus, Billy soaked in the quiet while he sat in the lounge sipping his pilfered JD and watched the mass exodus from the parking lot.

Nine days. It didn't seem that long, but it would feel like the longest nine days of his life.

He poured another whiskey, and began packing his gear. He was hitching a ride with whoever was heading to the hotel first.

The pocket door slid open with a bang. Cam burst into the bunk room, followed by the rest of his bandmates.

"You're not gonna fucking believe what just happened," Cam cried. "Rafe took a header off the stage. He's out cold. It looks like he broke his leg."

Billy straightened up. "Are you shitting me?"

"Nope," said Alan, their bass player. "He went to walk down the stairs from the back of the stage and missed them completely. I saw him. It was like he didn't even know where the fucking stairs were. He just stepped out into midair and down he went."

~

For once, the bus left on time. Only instead of going to the hotel, they were parked outside Cedars-Sinai. Exhausted and not getting any real updates, Billy, along with a few of the other band members, had given up sitting in the waiting room and returned to the bus to try and catch a few winks. It was close to eight in the morning when Carlos stepped into the bunk room, waking everyone, and ordering them into the main lounge. He looked like shit. Kev, who stood behind him, looked even worse.

"Okay," Carlos said, gripping a giant Styrofoam cup of coffee. "This is the four-one-one. Rafe's heading into surgery in about a half-hour. He's got two bad breaks in his right leg—one in the tibia and one in the fibula. They're going to have to insert a rod and pins . . ." He paused, took a long sip of his coffee, and continued. "I don't know what the fuck they're doing." He scrubbed a hand over his face, as if he could erase the exhaustion and frustration stamped there.

"Anyway, we're cancelling the rest of the tour until after the first of the year. And even that's up in the air, although Rafe's convinced he'll be up for the New Year's gig."

Carlos surveyed the collection of musicians standing before him.

"This afternoon's show is still on. Rafe insists since it's at the children's hospital. Truth Monkey can't perform, obviously. Pernicious Anemia, you guys will play both sets. After the show, head home, stay here. Do whatever the fuck you want. I've got my hands full right now, so you're on your own with travel arrangements. Just turn in your receipts and the tour will cover your expenses." With a warning glare, he aimed his finger at all of them. "Within reason. Don't be sending me no first-class shit."

He drained his coffee and tossed the empty cup into the sink.

"I'm heading to my bus so I can get a little shut-eye before the show this afternoon. Unless one of you falls and breaks your neck, don't anybody fucking bother me. We're pulling out in about ten minutes, so be ready to roll."

Grinning would have been a shitty thing to do. Billy was sorry Rafe had been hurt, but if that was his ticket home for Christmas, then hallelujah.

The remainder of Truth Monkey began packing up their bunks, all except Kev.

"Hey, rock star," he called as Billy returned to his bunk.

Billy eyed him narrowly. Kev had stayed clear of him for the past two days. Figures as soon as Rafe was indisposed, he'd start shit again.

"What the fuck do you want?"

"Hurry and pack your shit. There's a car on its way to pick you up and take you to the airport."

"In case you didn't hear, we have a gig this afternoon." He motioned to himself and the rest of his band.

"They do. You don't."

Billy zeroed in on Cam, whose face gave away nothing. What the fuck? Rafe, who had every right to insist on Billy being off the tour, had given him a free pass, and now his own band was giving him the boot.

"Are you firing me?"

Cam raised his hands. "No way! Let the man finish."

Kev pushed off the counter and took a step toward Billy.

"I'll fill in for you this afternoon so you can head home to your wife and kids." He thrust out his hand. "I owe you this, and I'm sorry for the shit I pulled with you the past few weeks. Maybe if I'd have worried more about what I had at home, I wouldn't be spending the holiday at my sister's as the weird uncle."

Billy hesitated, waiting to see if Kev was just yanking his chain, but the earnest look on his face convinced him that he was telling the truth. He accepted Kev's hand. "Nah. You'd be the weird uncle no matter what."

Kev laughed. "True, but at least I wouldn't be alone."

Kev was still a dick, but for this, Billy might actually let it go.

He looked at Cam, Alan, and Grayson, their rhythm player. "You all right with this? If you want me to stay, I'm here. I mean it."

"No fucking way," Cam said. "Take the man up on his offer. And seriously," he gave Kev a sour look. "This is the least he could do after pulling that shit."

Billy grabbed his jacket. "What about my guitars?"

"I got it covered," Kev insisted. "My tech will take care of getting your equipment to New York. Now get the fuck outta here. If you don't want to be hitching a ride on Santa's sleigh, you better get your ass moving."

CHAPTER 18

Billy rode to the airport in style. Kev had ordered a limo and although it was early enough in the day, traffic had been heavy, especially as they closed in on LAX. It gave him time to think, and after debating with himself for most of the ride, he decided not to call Katie. He wanted to surprise them. The look on their faces would make the strain of the last few weeks worthwhile.

He felt naked traveling without his guitars. With just one overstuffed duffle bag as a carry on, he could skip baggage claim when he landed and be home that much faster.

"Excuse me, sir. What airline?" the driver asked.

"Oh, shit. Um . . . drop me off at the Continental Terminal."

He didn't have a ticket, but he'd flown Continental into Newark from

LAX before. Why take a chance with one of the others and find out they only flew to JFK or LaGuardia?

The limo had barely stopped before he had the door open. "Merry Christmas," he called to the driver as he hopped out onto the curb to make his way into the crowded terminal.

He found the shortest line, still one of the longest he'd ever had to wait in, and inched along with what had to be the entire population of Southern California.

Forty minutes of piped-in holiday Muzak later, it was his turn. He dipped into his wallet and pulled out his credit card.

"Whatever you have available on the next flight to Newark."

The reservations clerk smiled and began clicking away on her keyboard.

"I can get you on a flight tomorrow leaving at 12:35 p.m. What credit card would you like to use?" She held out her hand.

His heart sank. "Tomorrow? I need a flight today."

"I'm sorry sir. All flights heading into Newark are full."

"What about first class? I don't care. I just need a ticket."

"I'm sorry. Tomorrow at 12:35 is the first available flight."

"Could you check if you have a seat on a flight to JFK then?"

"I'm sorry. We don't fly to JFK."

"Are you kidding?" The people in line behind him were beginning to grumble. "LaGuardia?"

"Sorry."

"You mean to tell me the only place you land on the East Coast is Newark?"

The louder his voice, the less she smiled.

"We also fly to Boston, Baltimore and to Dulles. Would you like me to check those flights for you, sir?"

"Won't do me any good if my truck is in Newark, will it?"

"I'm sorry, sir. The only other option, besides flying tomorrow, is to be put on standby."

Standby? It was better than tomorrow.

"Okay, fine. What are my chances of getting out of here today on standby?"

"Not good."

He pushed off the counter and dragged a hand through his hair. "Who else flies into Newark?"

"You might want to try TWA or United, but I'm sure they'll be booked as well. It is Christmas after all." She leaned around him. "May I help the next customer in line please?"

"Thanks for nothing," he muttered, pushing through the throng, which had only grown denser.

The next three hours were spent waiting in lines to find that TWA was booked solid. So was United, Southwest and U.S. Air. Delta and American, which only flew into JFK, had no flights until the following afternoon as well.

And he still didn't even have a ticket for tomorrow.

He trudged back to the Continental desk. At least there was still standby.

This time he only waited in line a half-hour. When he stepped in front of the same snarky bitch he'd dealt with earlier, her smile faded. He slapped his credit card onto the counter and pushed it toward her.

"Give me the first flight out of here to Newark, and I want to be on standby for whatever comes up before then."

She tapped away on her keyboard. "The first available flight leaves tomorrow at 7:30 p.m."

"What? You said it was around noon."

The bitch smiled. "Yes, I did. That was several hours ago. That flight is now booked."

His fucking head might just explode. "Fine. Whatever. Give me that one."

He waited while she completed his reservation and then handed him his ticket for Christmas night. So much for getting home for the holidays. The kids would be asleep before he even landed.

"I've added you to the standby list for the next three flights. The first flight leaves at 12:30 from Gate 72. You'll need to wait at the gate, and if there's a seat available, the clerk will call your name. The last flight out today is at eight, and the first one tomorrow, as you know, is at 12:35."

Billy tucked his ticket into the inside pocket of his leather jacket and stepped away from the counter. It was a little past eleven. All he'd had since last night's concert was a cup of stale hospital vending machine coffee. He needed to find something to eat. Then he planned to park himself in front of the gate and charm his way onto that plane.

~

So much for charm.

There were no seats available on the 12:35 p.m. flight, and the clerk at the gate had no interest in flirting with a long-haired musician who was, he'd noticed, in serious need of a shower. With nothing to do for the next seven hours, Billy sought out the least crowded bar, which turned out to be located in a restaurant on the south side of the airport in the Theme Building. Considering how packed the rest of the airport was, it was surprisingly empty. Only three other stools were occupied.

He climbed onto a stool at the end of the bar, set his duffle bag on the stool beside him and ordered a Jack Daniels on the rocks.

If he'd known he would spend the day in the airport, unable to get home, he would've just stayed and played the benefit. At least he would've been doing something that he loved, instead of sitting around feeling sorry for himself. He'd had enough of that over the past few weeks, and frankly, he was getting sick of it.

He picked up his drink stirrer and pushed an ice cube under the amber liquid and watched it bob back up to the surface. He lowered the stirrer back into the whiskey, pressed his index finger against the opening, lifted it, and let the liquid trickle over the ice cube. He did this a few more times, then tossed the stirrer onto the bar and drained his glass.

There had to be a better way to kill time.

"Another Jack Daniels?"

Billy pushed his glass toward the bartender. "Yep."

This would be his second drink. After everything that had happened in the past three weeks, he could easily drink himself stupid, but if he wanted to have any chance of finagling his way onto that plane tonight, he'd have to be sober.

If the plane took off without him, all bets were off.

He jabbed at the fresh ice cubes in his glass. Maybe after this he'd buy a book or a magazine—something to keep his mind occupied for the next few hours.

"Excuse me."

The man sitting a few stools away was speaking to him.

"Yeah?"

"Have we met?"

He didn't think so, but the guy could have been any one of dozens of record execs he'd met over the years. Mid-forties, neatly trimmed salt and pepper hair. Charcoal gray, pin-striped suit; silk tie; linen shirt; Rolex watch.

Fuck if he could remember.

Billy shook his head slowly, giving himself more time to think. "I'm not sure. It's possible."

The guy slid his drink over one stool closer, then followed it.

"Are you a musician?"

"I am."

"I thought so." He raised his glass. "Cheers."

Although he had no idea what they were toasting, Billy lifted his drink, tipped it in a small salute, and brought it to his lips.

"Heading home for the holidays?" the man asked, seeming to be in no hurry to identify himself, which put Billy in a bad position. How was he supposed to know if he could tell the guy to fuck off or not?

"That's the plan."

The man chuckled. "Doesn't sound like you're too sure about that."

Billy waved to the bartender. "You have any pretzels or peanuts or something?" The hot dog he'd had earlier wasn't cutting it, and if he had something to stuff in his mouth, he might not look like a good candidate for shooting the breeze with someone he may, or may not, know.

The bartender returned with a small bowl of peanuts.

"Make that two, will you?" said the man in the suit. He returned his focus to Billy. "So why do you seem unsure about heading home."

Was this guy serious? Judging by the sharpness of his gaze, Billy assumed that he was.

"That's because I can't get a flight out until tomorrow night. I'm hoping to go standby."

The guy tossed several peanuts in his mouth and chewed. "Tomorrow night? That sucks."

Billy sighed. "Yeah. It does."

"Are you still married?"

Billy's head snapped up. Who the fuck was this guy? Blue eyes, gray hair. There was something vaguely familiar about him, but whatever it was wasn't all that obvious.

"Yeah, I'm married. Tell me how we know each other, because to be honest, I'm having a hard time placing you."

The man shook his head and reached for another handful of peanuts. He cocked his head at Billy and snorted. "Figures."

Now he was just pissing him off.

"Look, dude. I meet a lot of people in my line of work, so if you're bummed that I don't remember you, I'm sorry."

"Bummed? Yeah, you could say I'm *bummed*. You'd think when a guy is responsible for destroying someone's relationship they might have a clue who it is they were hurting, but I guess guys like you do it all the time and don't give a damn who gets in their way."

Who the fuck was this? Billy slammed his drink onto the bar. "Look. I'm pretty sure I don't know you, and I'm positive I had nothing to do with your relationship. Trust me. I've been married for over six years. And if it was before that, I have no recollection."

"That's not what my fiancée—sorry—ex-fiancée said."

"Well, your ex-fiancée is a liar." Billy reached into his wallet and threw a twenty on the bar. He wasn't in the mood to sit there and argue with this nutcase all afternoon.

"I might have to disagree with you there. Christa is many things, but a liar? I'm not so sure. When I confronted her, she didn't hesitate to tell me about your little backroom tête-à-tête."

Billy dropped back onto his stool. *Barry Stifel.*

No wonder he had him confused with record execs, which he would naturally associate with Christa, his former agent. But Barry wasn't in the business. He was a CEO of some big firm on Wall Street.

Billy wanted to defend himself, but what could he say?

Yeah, your fiancée went down on me, but I was so out of it, I didn't even know what was happening.

That would probably earn him a broken nose, or at least the guy might attempt it. Not that Billy didn't deserve it in some way, but he wouldn't stand there and take it either.

"I should bust you right in the mouth for that," Barry said. There was little emotion, if any, behind the threat. "But to be honest, you probably saved me a lot of money in the long run. I can't imagine the marriage would have had any staying power and, knowing Christa, she'd have gone after every penny I had."

Billy didn't know what to say. What he wanted was to get the hell out of there. Fast. He drained his drink and set the empty glass on the bar, then reached for his duffle bag.

Barry motioned to the bartender. "Another Tanqueray and tonic, and whatever my friend is having over there." He pointed at Billy.

Billy shook his head. "No, thanks."

"I insist." Barry's eyes were like two chips of ice. If he'd been pouring the drink himself, Billy would have been afraid to drink it.

"You can insist all you wa—"

"You never told me if you were still married." Barry gave his gin and tonic a stir and tossed the stick on the bar. "You said you were married, but that doesn't mean it's to the same girl I met a few years ago. I assume guys like you go through them pretty fast."

Billy's jaw was so tense he thought he might crack a tooth.

"Pretty little thing. Very young, right?"

He nodded. "Katie."

"She must be very forgiving. Good for her."

He had to end this. Now. Barry could cause him some serious damage. Billy sat back down, and leaned closer. "Listen, Barry. I'm sorry about what happened. It's a shitty thing for me to say, but I can't take full responsibility. I didn't initiate it. And if I hadn't been so fucked up, it never would've happened. Unfortunately, I didn't stop it either. You wanna take a swing at me, that's your prerogative. I'm not one for standing back and letting people throw punches, even if I might deserve it. So be forewarned. But if it makes you feel any better, I've sacrificed much of my career thanks to Christa."

Barry gave his drink a swirl and laughed. "That doesn't even make sense."

"At the risk of you taking a swing at me anyway, if you knew Christa well enough to be engaged to her, then you know how vindictive she can be. She's had me by the short hairs. She's done everything in her power to cut me off at the knees whenever she can. When I was signed with her, I was inches away from my first recording contract. That all disappeared when I fired her. I work my ass off just to get by. Why the fuck do you think I'm on the other side of the country on Christmas Eve? The only reason I'm here is because my tour was postponed. Otherwise, I wouldn't see my family until after the holidays. And at the rate I'm going, I'll be spending Christmas in this fucking airport. So if you want to know if I regret what happened with Christa, damn straight. If I'd had a clear head, it never would've happened."

Billy snatched up his whiskey and shot it back. Then he stood and reached for his duffle bag.

"Leaving?" Barry asked.

"Yeah. I'm on standby for an eight o'clock flight."

Barry looked at his Rolex. "It's quarter after one."

"I can't sit here and drink all afternoon. I'll leave you in peace. Merry Christmas."

He'd just about reached the door when it opened and an elegant blonde strolled in. She smiled when she saw him, but her eyes lit up when they found their target.

"There you are!" she cried, rushing toward Barry as he stood to greet her. He stood and wrapped his arms around her. Billy had almost cleared the door when Barry called out to him.

"Billy wait. I'd like you to meet my fiancée."

Barry looked at the woman in his arms the same way Billy believed he looked at Katie. "Amber, this is Billy McDonald. He's an old friend of mine."

Billy stepped forward and held out his hand. "It's nice to meet you."

"It's nice to meet you, too. Where are you headed?" she asked.

"Same place we are," Barry answered. Then he looked at Billy and smiled. "Isn't that a coincidence?"

CHAPTER 19

"So women just drop to their knees and offer to . . . you know . . . service you?"

Barry watched his fiancée with an amused expression. Billy just cringed, especially since her attention on him hadn't wavered since Barry's private jet, a Gulfwing IV, had obtained cruising altitude. And with every glass of champagne she downed, the questions became more personal and uncomfortable.

"I, um . . ." How the hell was he supposed to answer a question like that? He no longer accepted any *servicing*, but he couldn't deny that it happened. Especially when Amber had asked Barry how he and Billy had met, and the bastard told her—in excruciating detail— how Billy had been the one responsible for the destruction of his and Christa's engagement. Amber had squealed with delight and declared Christa a slut. Billy had been glad she was confined to her chair with a seatbelt, or she probably would have flung herself at him as a thank you for putting Barry back on the market.

It had been the most uncomfortable takeoff he'd ever experienced, and the ride itself was no picnic. He would have been better off in the luggage hold or strapped to a wing.

"And what about women? Are men as willing to offer oral sex to a woman? Say, like Madonna?"

"I don't know Madonna."

She turned to Barry. "Darling? What do you think?"

"I don't know Madonna either."

She gave him a playful shove. "I mean women like Madonna, performers. Do you think it's the same for them as it is for men?"

"I honestly wouldn't know."

"Billy?"

Billy shrugged. *Why didn't I buy a book when I had the chance?* He yawned, but she wasn't deterred. The elegant woman who had glided into the bar to meet Barry a couple of hours earlier seemed to have disappeared. And given her curiosity about the sex lives of musicians, Barry would be a fool if he ever let her out of his sight at a rock concert.

Amber finished the last of her champagne and signaled for the stewardess to bring her another. If Katie had that much champagne, she'd be curled up against him, sound asleep. Amber, on the other hand, was getting more revved up with every glass.

Katie. He could almost feel the heat of her body beside him. Tonight, he'd sleep, holding her in his arms. If he could hold on to that image, it might make Amber's incessant yammering more tolerable.

"So, Billy." Amber waved her refilled glass in his direction. "Exactly how many women would you say you've had sex with?" She helped herself to a stuffed mushroom, which distracted her for about a second. "Oh, yum. These are delicious. Billy, have a mushroom." She leaned forward and attempted to pop one in his mouth. He plucked it from her fingers just in time.

Barry no longer looked amused. Billy prayed for turbulence. Amber was undeterred.

She nudged Billy's shin with the toe of her high heeled boot. "Now where was I? Oh. Sex. Now think about it before you answer. Is a blow job the same as having sex? Or is it just something you come to expect? What about if you go down on a woman? Or does it have to be the old hide the salami—"

"Amber, darling . . ."

Finally!

"I think that's enough questions for now."

Barry was looking more uncomfortable than amused.

Amber reached for another mushroom. "Billy doesn't mind, do you?"

She didn't give him a chance to answer. If she had, he would have asked where the parachutes were.

"Besides, I find this fascinating." She ran a perfectly manicured finger over Barry's cheek, and continued down his neck. "And even a little sexy." She grabbed his tie and gave it a sharp yank, pulling him toward her. "Don't you?" She ran her tongue over Barry's bottom lip.

That's it.

Billy stood. "Would you mind if I stepped into the bathroom and washed up? With all the commotion after the concert, and then trying to get to the airport on time, I didn't get a chance to shower, and I would really like to freshen up before heading home, if that's okay."

Especially if you two are about to renew your membership in the mile-high club.

"Not at all," Barry waved him off. "Take your time."

Oh, I intend to.

They'd be lucky if they would see him again before they landed at Teterboro.

CHAPTER 20

A fire crackled in the fireplace. A large bowl of popcorn waited on the coffee table. All Kate had to do was cue up "Mr. Magoo's Christmas Carol," a childhood favorite she'd passed on to her own children. She'd made hot cocoa from scratch, complete with mini-marshmallows and whipped cream. For dinner they'd had hotdogs and beans at Devin's request and chicken fingers at Rhiannon's request. And they were all dressed in coordinating holiday pajamas. But with Billy's matching PJ bottoms folded in the bottom drawer of his dresser, it didn't feel like Christmas Eve.

"When's Daddy gonna call?" Rhiannon asked.

Good question. Kate hadn't heard from Billy since a day earlier, before the show in LA. It was a little after eight, which meant it was around five in

California. The benefit would be over by now. He was probably on the bus, heading to wherever it was they were going. She assumed he'd call when he got settled in his hotel, but he should know the kids would be waiting to talk to him.

Despite missing their father, they were still excited about Santa coming. Getting them to fall asleep wouldn't be easy, so she decided to let them stay up and hoped that they'd nod off during the movie—even if she'd have to carry them up to bed.

Billy had been gone since the end of November, and she missed him every day, but tonight would be the worst.

She tucked her feelings away, along with the quilt she secured around her and her children, Rhiannon on one end, her on the other, and Devin in the middle.

"Daddy had to play a benefit for sick children today, remember? And since the time is different where he is, it's still early there. I'm sure he'll call us in a little while." She set the bowl of popcorn on Devin's lap and started the VCR. "I bet he calls during our favorite part of the movie." She changed her voice to make it sound like it would be a very bad thing. "What's your favorite part, buddy?" she asked Devin.

He giggled. "When they sing razzleberry dressing!"

"That's my favorite part, too."

Kate twirled a finger through one of her daughter's curls. "What about you, sweetie?"

Rhiannon sipped her cocoa, giving much thought to question. "I think I like the scary part best."

"I don't like the scary part," Devin answered.

Kate moved closer. "Well then, we'll just have to cuddle more during the scary part, okay?"

With the room lights dim, it was impossible to miss the beam of headlights coming up the driveway. People often mistook their long driveway for a road, and would end up pulling around behind their house, turn around, and leave. It still made her uncomfortable, especially when Billy wasn't home. She set her cocoa on the end table and watched for the tail lights.

Instead, there was a knock on the front door.

She flipped back the quilt, then tucked the edges around Devin.

"You guys watch the movie. I'm going to see who that is."

"Maybe it's Santa," Devin crowed, trying to scramble out from under the blanket.

"Or Daddy!" Rhiannon was about to follow.

"Santa doesn't knock and neither does Daddy. Watch the movie. I'll be right back."

It was probably Eileen or Marty. But still. A knock on the door this late on Christmas Eve was unsettling. She pulled back the curtain in the hall. The police car idling in her driveway, set her heart to racing.

She rushed into the dining room and tore open the front door.

The officer had his back to her, but she knew who it was before he turned.

His thumbs were hooked in his utility belt. A gun was holstered on his right hip and a radio on his shoulder. Kate had never had a run-in with the police—not even a ticket—but seeing one on her doorstep, even Digger, made her stomach twist.

"Digger? What's wrong?" She spoke through the locked screen door.

His eyes dropped to her red plaid pajamas and shot back up again. Kate wrapped her arms around herself, feeling exposed and wishing she'd been wearing a robe, even though she was covered from her neck to her ankles in flannel.

"Nothing's wrong. I'm just patrolling tonight, and I knew you would be home alone. I just thought I'd check in, make sure everything's all right."

She'd been alone many times over the past few years, and not once had a Belleville police officer ventured up her driveway to check on her. Of course she didn't know any of them personally. She vacillated between being touched by Digger's concern and a little creeped out.

"That's very sweet of you, but we're fine. The kids and I are watching a movie." She lowered her voice. "Once I get them off to bed, I get to do the Santa thing."

He cleared his throat. "Need any help? I can't cook, but I am good at putting stuff together. I get off at eleven. I can come back, after your kids are asleep."

She felt her smile start to slip. "Thanks, Digger. But that's not—"

"I just want you to know, Kate, if you were my wife, I wouldn't be traipsing around the country and leaving you by yourself in the woods with two kids. Especially not over Christmas. You deserve better than that."

Her body stiffened. "First of all, this is hardly the woods." She fixed a smile back on her face and did her damnedest to hide her annoyance. "And second, who told you we were alone?" Billy's touring schedule wasn't a secret, but neither of them went around broadcasting it either.

Digger screwed up his face like he believed it was a foolish question. And at first, she didn't think he was going to answer.

"My mother. She spoke with your mother the other day. She told her she was supposed to come because your husband was gone and she didn't want you to be alone again. She's worried about you and . . . you know." The way he cocked his head Kate assumed Billy was "you know." She wanted to scream. It wasn't Digger's fault that her mother was spewing fake concern and making it sound like Kate had a horrible marriage and a philandering husband.

"I'm touched by your kindness, Digger, I am, but—ooph!"

Devin barreled into her at full speed, wrapping his arms around her thighs.

"Hey! A policeman," he cried. "Cool!"

Kate reached down and lifted him up.

"Hey, bud. What's your name?" Digger asked.

Suddenly shy, Devin buried his face in her neck. "This is Devin," she answered, "and Rhiannon is in the other room. I really should get back to her."

"Yeah, sure. If you need anything, Kate, just call. Like I said, I'm on till eleven, but even after, they can get a message to me. Or maybe I should give you my number."

"Mommm!" Rhiannon tugged on Kate's sleeve. "I don't wanna watch by myself." She gave Digger an evil look.

"I'm sorry, Digger. I really have my hands full, but thanks again. And I promise, if I need anything, I'll call the station. Nine-one-one, right?" She tapped her temple. "Got it right here."

He took a step back. "Yeah, good. Okay then. Merry Christmas." Kate started to close the door. "Hope Santa's good to you guys."

Devin leaned so far out to answer, Kate had to let go of the door and hold onto him to keep him from falling. "He's going to bring me a train set. Do you like trains?"

"I love trains."

This could go on all night.

"Say 'Merry Christmas,' Dev. The nice policeman has to go and you have to go to bed."

Rhiannon stomped her foot. "I'm not going to bed until Daddy calls. We haven't talked to him for days!"

Kate pulled her daughter away from the door. "It hasn't been days." She looked at Digger and shook her head. "It hasn't been days." The fact that she felt the need to repeat herself to Digger was irritating. She put Devin down and again started to close the door. "Seriously. I've got to get these two to bed so Santa can come."

Digger took two more steps back. "Okay. I'll see you. Remember. Call me."

She nodded. Why, she had no idea. She had no intention of calling him. At this point, she probably wouldn't even call him if she actually needed a police officer. So much for trying to fix him up with Pam.

He was still watching her from the porch as she snapped the door shut and locked it.

She slumped against the wall. Between Billy being gone, and then not hearing from him since early yesterday, Digger showing up like some lovesick hero, and her mother talking about her and acting as if she were actually concerned about anything going on Kate's life, Kate was feeling more than a little overwhelmed. With Devin and Rhiannon looking at her expectantly, there was no giving into it.

"C'mon. Let's finish watching the movie, and then you can hang up your stockings and put out some milk and cookies for Santa, and then bed."

"I wanna cookie." Devin tugged on the leg of her pajamas.

"Okay. How about we make up a plate for Santa now? You can each have one cookie."

Kate took out the Santa plate and let Devin and Rhiannon each put two cookies on the plate—which meant she'd be eating four cookies later—then she poured a half-glass of milk. Devin carried the milk into the living room, followed by Rhiannon with the cookies.

"How is Santa going to come down the chimney without getting burned?" Devin asked as he set the glass on the hearth.

"I'll let the fire go out," Kate promised, "and if it isn't out by the time he comes, he can put it out, so don't worry."

They scrambled back onto the couch and Kate began to rewind the movie to the halfway point, which was around the time Digger showed up. As the VCR tape whirred backwards, there was a thump overhead. Just what she needed, squirrels in the attic again. The second thump was louder. That was one big-ass squirrel.

If she wasn't twenty-five years old, she would've thought it was—

"Santa!" Devin fought his way out from under the quilt.

There was another loud thump. Something or someone was definitely on the roof. And since she no longer believed in flying reindeer, she wondered if it was Digger trying to ingratiate himself with her and her children.

Goddamn it, Mother.

Kate threw back the quilt. "It's probably a squirrel. I'm going to go check."

"No! What if it's Santa? You'll scare him away."

That's the plan.

"It's not Santa. He won't come if you're still awake. The movie is almost over. Finish watching it and then you're going to bed."

"Not until Daddy calls!"

"Rhiannon, you're going to bed. Daddy will call in the morning. He's waiting so you can tell him what Santa brings you."

"That's not what you said before. You said he'd call."

For a six-year-old, Rhiannon had a memory like an elephant. "I forgot. He said he'd call tomorrow. It's after nine. He probably thinks you're already asleep, that's why he didn't call."

There was another loud thump and the three of them looked at the ceiling. Devin shimmied off the couch.

"I want to see the big squirrel."

"It's cold and it's starting to snow. Get back on the couch and watch the movie. When I come back inside, you're going to bed." *And I'm having a great big glass of wine. Maybe a whole bottle.*

She tugged a knit hat over her ears, slipped into her jacket, and pulled on her boots. At this point, if Digger was on her roof, she might just throw something at him. Of course it might not be Digger. Her hand rested on the back door. If she called the police, and it wasn't Digger, that meant he'd come back. And if it was just an animal of some kind, she'd feel pretty silly.

Marty! It was probably Marty trying to be Santa for the kids. This was exactly something he would do, and he had a Santa suit. She rushed out into the snow before the crazy fool could fall off her roof.

Snow crunched under her feet, but otherwise, there was no sound. A sliver of a moon hung in the sky, leaving a black velvet canopy, studded with thousands of stars. Kate looked up, her breath hanging in the air about her head, and shivered. The main part of the house was two stories, but the living room was only one, which made it easy enough to reach the roof. She picked her way through the snow until she was able to get a good view of the roof.

Although it was dark, she could still see that the snow on the roof had been disturbed. Something had been up there. As she moved closer, a leg hooked over the ridge, followed by a body—a body dressed from head to toe in red.

"Hey!" she called out in a whispered yell, hopefully just loud enough for Santa. If Rhiannon and Devin thought Santa was on the roof, they'd be outside in a flash—probably barefoot.

A head popped up, but she must have startled the intruder, because he lost his grip and began sliding over the other side. As he disappeared from view, she heard a very loud, very familiar, "Fuck!"

"Oh my God!" Kate ran to the front of the house as fast as she could in six inches of snow. Santa was clinging to the roof ridge and scrambling to find his footing. A ladder leaned against the side of the house.

"Billy?"

He looked down. "Hey, babe."

"What are you doing? Are you drunk?"

"No!"

"Then what the hell are you doing on the roof? Get down before you break your neck."

"I wanted to surprise you."

"I'm surprised. I'm also freezing." He shimmied across the roof toward the ladder. As she stood below it to steady it, two small faces peered out the window at her.

"We have an audience," she said as Billy climbed down the ladder.

He skipped the last two steps, jumping into the snow beside her, grinning. "I don't care." He stepped toward the window and waved. She could hear their excited screams through the glass.

"They'll be out here in two seconds," she warned.

"I have to do something first." He cupped her face in his white-gloved hands. Then he bent and kissed her. And in that kiss, she could feel all the emotion and sadness she'd heard from him over the past few weeks pouring out of him. He kissed her for so long and so hard, she no longer felt the cold air wrapping itself around her legs. She wrapped her arms around his waist, and when she heard shouts of "Daddy! Daddy!" coming from the front porch, he finally pulled back. There were tears in her eyes, but she laughed.

"Welcome home, Santa. Merry Christmas."

"It sure as fuck is now."

She kissed him again. "How? Why? Did you get fired?"

"No, I didn't get fired. First I want to get inside and get my hands on those little buggers, and then I want to get my hands all over you, and then I'll tell you how and why. Deal?"

"Deal."

"Good." His face grew serious. "And after that, you can tell me why there was a cop here a few minutes ago hitting on my wife."

CHAPTER 21

Between the excitement of Santa's impending visit and Billy's unexpected homecoming, getting Rhiannon and Devin to go to bed was nearly impossible. It took Kate telling them she thought she heard sleigh bells, and if they didn't go to sleep soon, Santa might have to skip their house, before they willingly agreed to stay in their beds. Even then, it took lots of cuddles and kisses from their father before they were finally, blissfully, asleep.

Kate watched from the doorway of Devin's room as Billy, still dressed as Santa, dropped one last kiss on his sleeping son's forehead.

"At least they'll sleep in tomorrow," he whispered as he joined her in the hall, looking like he was down for the count as well.

She chuckled as he rested his hands on her waist. "Doubtful. It's

Christmas. They'll probably be up even earlier than usual. And since you must be exhausted, you should probably head to bed as well."

He pulled her tighter, and she melted into the warmth of him.

"No way. I've missed too much already these last few weeks. I'm dressed for duty. I've got stockings to fill and presents to put under the tree." His lips ghosted the sensitive spot behind her ear and goosebumps sprang up along her arm. "And then there's that whole business about doing Mommy underneath the mistletoe."

"Kissing," she whispered. "Kissing Mommy underneath the mistletoe."

His lips moved lower. Despite the chill of the upstairs hallway, her body was heating up. If they kept this up, it would be plenty hard to fulfill Santa's duties anytime soon.

"Oh, there'll be kissing all right." He backed her away from the door to Devin's room and against the wall in the hallway, his hardness pressing up against her belly. There would definitely be more than kissing.

She gave a little tug on the thick vinyl belt cinched around his waist.

"So, Santa. Where's your little round belly? You're pretty buff for a jolly old elf."

"There's nothing elf-like about me," said her six foot four inch husband, "and if Santa had abs like mine, he wouldn't stuff his shirt either."

She pressed her face against his chest to keep her laugh from waking the kids. "I see Santa's also modest. But I have to agree. I think if mothers around the world had any idea you might be coming down their chimneys, they'd be leaving more than milk and cookies under their trees."

"The only thing I want under the tree tonight is you. And I ain't waiting until morning to unwrap you."

As the blood pumping through her veins began to heat up, the flannel pajamas that had seemed so cozy earlier, had to go.

She gave his ass a tight squeeze. "Why don't you go play Santa, and I'll meet you downstairs in a few minutes. I have one more gift to wrap."

Kate's mother had sent wrapped gifts for Devin and Rhiannon, but for Kate, she'd sent money. Since she hadn't mentioned Billy specifically, Kate had assumed it was meant for both of them, but knowing her mother, she'd probably excluded him on purpose.

Which is why she felt less guilty spending the entire two hundred dollars on one trip to Victoria's Secret, even though all she'd bought was a boned corset with matching burgundy and black satin panties and a thigh-length robe.

She stood in the doorway to the living room with a large satin bow in her hair, and holding a bottle of wine and two glasses while Billy stoke the fire. He'd stripped out of his Santa suit, and was wearing nothing but a pair of black boxers and his Santa hat.

"Nice outfit," she said as she sauntered into the room.

He turned, brushing the dirt from the firewood off his hands. "I could say the same about you. Holy shit, Mrs. Claus."

Kate set the bottle and glasses on the coffee table, next to the leftover bowl of popcorn.

When she straightened up, Billy tugged the ribbon from her hair. He motioned to the outfit.

"Is this my Christmas gift from you?"

"Actually, this," she did a little turn, giving him the full effect, "is from my mother. What's under it is from me."

He blanched. "Your mother bought this for you?"

"No. She sent me money. I used it to buy something I thought you'd enjoy."

He waggled his eyebrows and settled his hands on her waist. "You got that right." His mouth traveled slowly, planting soft, open-mouthed kisses along her shoulder and up her neck and jaw. "Thank you, Evelyn," he murmured, his breath hot against her skin. "But that's enough about your mother. I've got a raging hard-on, and I'm sure as fuck not going to let her kill it."

His hand thrust into her hair, gripping it, and pulling her head back. When his mouth covered hers her knees almost buckled. It had only been three weeks, and there'd been times when he'd been away much longer than this, but she couldn't remember a sweeter homecoming.

She ran her tongue along his bottom lip and giggled. "Did you just eat a candy cane?"

"Hmmm. Maybe," he purred against her ear.

She pulled back.

"Are you hungry?" she asked, not wanting to stop what had just started, but trying to be a good wife.

His eyes were almost navy as he gripped her ass and hoisted her up until she could wrap her legs around his waist.

"I'm hungry, all right. For you."

"Ditto."

"I didn't think it was even possible, but I can't remember ever wanting you more than I do right now," he said, moving across the living room.

"Me, too," she said as he lay her on the sofa, her voice low and breathy. She shimmied out of the satin robe and dropped it onto the floor. Her fingers snaked through his hair, soft and silky, and pulled him closer. He smelled . . . spicy. She buried her head in his neck and sniffed.

"If you've been traveling since early this morning, why do you smell like you just had a shower?"

"Because I washed up." He rose up onto his knees and hooked his fingers into her panties, tugging them down her legs. He gave them a toss and they landed on a branch of the artificial tree in the corner. "On the plane."

She struggled to sit up. "In an airplane bathroom?" The thought of her extra-tall husband taking a sponge bath in an extra-tiny airplane bathroom seemed inconceivable.

His teeth sank into her ankle, followed by a kiss, and then the tip of his tongue.

"Do you want to discuss my hellish morning and afternoon or would you rather wait until tomorrow to do that and make up for the last three weeks tonight?"

She tried to answer, but when he sucked her big toe into his mouth she had a hard time finding her words. Instead, she just groaned and shook her head.

"That's what I thought."

He worked his way up from her ankle, along the inside of her calf, planting kisses along the way, stopping when he reached partway up her thigh. His finger trailed under the edge of her bustier.

"I know I don't have the patience to figure out how this comes off, so unless you want this to be the one and only time you get to wear it—and that would be a shame, because it looks fucking amazing on you—I suggest you get it off. Now."

He didn't have to tell her twice. Raising her arm, she reached for the side zipper and gave it a gentle tug, and watched the lustful look spread across Billy's face.

Before she could drop it on the floor, he snatched it from her hands and sent it sailing in the same direction as her panties.

"On second thought, this," he waved his hands over her now naked body, "is fucking amazing."

She reached for his briefs, but he caught her wrist.

"Not yet. You first. I'm afraid once he's unleashed, there's going to be no holding back, and I need to worship you first." He lowered his body to hers, the heat of his smooth skin warming her instantly, and when his thumb found her center and a long finger dipped inside her, her eyes rolled back inside her head. By the time he added a second finger, her body had begun to quiver.

"Oh god, Billy," she whimpered. As his teeth sank into her shoulder she exploded around him.

She could barely catch her breath, but she reached for him, grabbing through the thin cotton fabric of his briefs. Given the rock-hard pulsing beneath her fingers, she didn't think he'd be able to wait much longer.

"I need you inside me. Now. Please," she begged, returning the favor and catching his nipple in her teeth, giving it a gentle tug.

"Fuck," he groaned, raising up and stripping off his underwear.

"Leave the hat," she ordered as he climbed between her legs and sank into her with a throaty groan. "Who knows when I'll get to have sex with Santa again?"

CHAPTER 22

"So you want to tell me why you smell like spice and sandalwood?"

Billy pressed a kiss beneath Kate's ear. She wiggled closer, under his arm, in their bed, right where he wanted her. He should have been on the other side of the country in a Hollywood hotel room, alone on Christmas Eve. Talk about Christmas miracles.

"It's a long story and it's late." He brushed his hand along the side of her face, illuminated by the candle glowing in the front window, the one he'd asked her to leave on for him. She yawned, but persisted.

"You said you washed up on the plane. Since when is there enough room in an airplane bathroom to get clean enough to smell this good?" She pressed her face against his chest. "You smell amazing."

"Private planes have nice-sized bathrooms, not to mention, top of the line French soaps and Egyptian cotton."

"The tour chartered you a private plane so you could come home?"

"Ha! Nice try. Carlos didn't have time to make travel arrangements, let alone charter a plane. I was on my own. Cam, Alan, and Grayson are still in L.A. They had to play the benefit, but Truth Monkey's lead guitarist offered to fill in for me so that I could head home."

"Kev Cunningham? Wow. Cam and the other guys didn't mind?"

"No. They knew how low I've been feeling, so they were cool with it. Kev lives in L.A., so he was probably home long before me."

Kate slipped her leg between his and snuggled in closer. "That was really nice of him. I hope I get to thank him in person someday."

Not if he could help it. As far as Billy was concerned, she'd never get anywhere near Kev Cunningham or any of the guys in Truth Monkey. After the way Kev had been running his mouth on the bus, Billy wasn't sure if he even wanted her near his own band again. There was no way he could risk her ever finding out about Christa. No fucking way.

"So tell me how you ended up on a private plane." The last of her sentence was swallowed up in a yawn.

"You're tired. I'm tired—"

"No I'm not. Besides, I'm afraid to fall asleep and then wake up and find out I was dreaming."

God, this woman. What had he possibly done to deserve her? He planted several kisses on the top of her head.

"You're not dreaming. When I got to LAX, all the flights home were booked. The earliest I could get a ticket was tomorrow night, and I was having no luck on standby. I had a few hours between flights, so I was sitting in the bar and this guy tells me I look familiar." He swallowed hard, wanting to plow through the next part as quickly as possible. "Turns out, I knew his ex-fiancée. He felt sorry for me, not having a flight home, and he and his girlfriend offered me a ride on his Gulfstream."

"Who's his ex?" Kate asked, yawning.

He dropped his voice, not wanting to answer. "Christa Dunphy."

"Humph. I wonder why he and Christa broke up. She seemed like the type who'd want her own plane."

Billy averted his eyes as easily as he danced around the truth.

"I think he saw her for what she really was. Can't say I blame him."

"Guess not. I hate to say it, but I never liked her. She's not very nice."

He ran his hand along Kate's back, lightly running his nails along her soft skin, knowing how much she loved when he did that and hoping she'd try to sleep. "You're right. She's not." He tipped her face up to his and kissed her softly. "You need to sleep and so do I. The kids will be up before we know it, and other than a brief nap on the ride from Teterboro to Newark to pick up my truck, I've been up for nearly forty hours." She wiggled against him. "Although I promise, if you press against me like that one more time, neither of us will be getting any sleep."

Her chuckle was almost evil, more so when she swirled her tongue over his naked pec. "Is that a promise?"

"It is, you wicked woman."

Her answer was a yawn, muffled by her face pressing against his chest.

"You win," she said, "but only because I'm certain the kids will have us up in just a few hours."

"They'll sleep in," he said, stifling a yawn of his own. "Trust me."

She gave his nipple a light tweak. "Oh, you silly, silly boy."

CHAPTER 23

"Oomph!"

Hard to believe, but at only forty five pounds, Devin was the first to knock the wind out of Billy in more than twenty years. His four-year-old face swam in front of Billy's bleary eyes.

"Wake up!" Devin yelled, sharpening Billy's focus. Kate groaned, her head buried under her pillow.

Rhiannon tugged at the covers, but he snagged them from her in the nick of time. Good thing, given he and Katie hadn't bothered to slip into their Christmas PJs when they'd hit the sheets. Or any PJs for that matter.

Kate dragged her head out from under her pillow. She looked so deliciously tousled, he hated having to get up, although it was Christmas, and he'd wanted to be home for this exact moment.

"Go plug in the lights on the tree and Daddy and I will be right behind you," she said, her voice so low and sexy with sleep, his morning wood grew stiffer.

"Don't run!" she shouted to the tiny footfalls pounding down the narrow staircase.

"I need a gallon of coffee." She rolled into his arms. "What time is it?"

Gray dawn was visible outside the window, meaning the sun still hadn't risen. He fished for his watch on the nightstand.

"Six forty three."

She slipped her head under the covers. "Make that two gallons."

"C'mon, Sleeping Beauty. I warned you last night, but you had to have your way with me."

She grabbed the skin around his waist and pinched.

"Uh, unh. Payback's a bitch." He gave the sheets and blanket a hard tug. That got her moving.

Kate squealed, grabbing fruitlessly. "Ack! You're so mean. I'm freezing!"

He slapped her ass playfully. "Then you better get up and get dressed. Santa came." He grabbed the hat on the nightstand and fixed it atop his head, and then reached for the plaid flannel pajama bottoms that matched his son's. Kate shivered as she pulled on a similar pair.

"How about you go put a fire in the fireplace, and I'll get the coffee going, and if you're lucky, I'll figure out how to hook up an IV for us right to the pot."

"Sounds good." He waited until she buttoned the last button on her pajama top, then he bent down and kissed her.

"Merry Christmas, baby."

Smiling up at him, she looped her arms around his waist and pressed her chin into his chest. "Merry Christmas."

CHAPTER 24

Kate aimed the video camera at her daughter, anxious to capture the moment when she opened the present she'd been begging for; the one Kate had sworn she would not be buying: an American Girl doll, with blond hair and blue eyes. She'd broken her own promise not to buy it, but when it looked like Billy wouldn't be home for Christmas, she'd wanted to soften her children's' disappointment any way she could. So, Santa had delivered the doll overnight, while Devin would be receiving an equally expensive collection of his favorite: Legos.

"What do you think it is, Ree?" Billy asked as Rhiannon excitedly tore at the red and green paper Kate used only for gifts from Santa.

"I think it's my American Girl doll. The one that looks just like me."

Billy looked at Kate and winked.

"I don't think so, sweetie. Mommy said Santa doesn't have any of those dolls, remember?"

Rhiannon lowered the partially unwrapped package and huffed at her father.

"Mommy's never been to the North Pole, so how would she know?"

Kate swallowed a laugh. Rhiannon had a bit of an attitude for a six-year-old, and the last thing she wanted to do was encourage her, but sometimes, the kid was downright funny. Besides, she hated scolding her, especially on Christmas, and certainly not when she was about to get exactly what she'd asked for.

The last of the paper fell away, and Rhiannon let go a scream that might have reached the North Pole.

"It is! It is!" she cried, fumbling with the box. Unable to get it open, she thrust it at her father while she danced around the room, crowing with excitement. Kate chewed on her lip, desperate to keep from tearing up. Being able to give her children something they'd so desperately wanted would never grow old, even if her better judgment had insisted it was an extravagant gift. Growing up, Kate couldn't remember receiving much of anything on her list to Santa. Her gifts had been sensible and practical. She felt Rhiannon's excitement as much, if not more so, than if the present had been her own heart's desire, which at that moment, was slicing through the packaging to remove their daughter's doll.

While Billy removed the last strap holding the doll in her box, Rhiannon spun around, planted her little hands on her tiny hips, and informed Kate of how wrong she'd been about Santa's having any American Girl dolls.

"Yeah, Mommy," Billy said, cocking an eyebrow in her direction. "I'm surprised about that one too."

Kate shrugged and smiled. "What can I say? I guess I was wrong."

"I guess so," he mumbled, setting Rhiannon's new treasure into her waiting arms.

It was Devin's turn next, and he ripped at the brightly colored paper with both hands.

"What is it?" he cried, as excited as Rhiannon had been with her doll.

"It's a T-ball set," Kate answered. "You'll be old enough to play this spring. Now you can practice. And if you like it, maybe you can play Little League when you get a bit older."

"Cool!" He said, eyeing the picture on the box. "Will you teach me, Dad?"

Billy stared at the box in his son's hand, his face blank. "Maybe. We'll see."

A flush of disappointment filled her, but Kate let it go. It was Christmas.

"You know what? If Daddy isn't around to teach you, I will," she said. "It'll be fun. Me, you and Rhiannon can play. Okay?"

"I don't like T-ball," Rhiannon said, following up with an indignant sniff.

"Let's not worry about that now," Billy said. "You have more presents to open. Ree? It's your turn."

She reached for a package that Kate didn't recognize. "This one's from you, Daddy."

"It sure is."

Billy slid over beside Kate as Rhiannon ripped a velvet ribbon off the foil-wrapped package.

"Fancy," Kate said.

"Yeah, sorry about this."

"Sorry about wh—"

A screech nearly pierced her eardrum.

"Look, Mommy, look! Daddy got me an American Girl doll."

Kate felt her jaw go slack.

Billy leaned in. "You said you weren't getting it, and I felt bad about not being here for Christmas," he whispered, "so I ordered the damn doll and had it sent ahead to the theater we played in Portland."

When she got over the initial shock of Rhiannon now having two dolls, Kate had to admit that it really was a thoughtful thing for him to do.

"You're a good daddy." She kissed him on his bare shoulder. "And aren't you freezing?"

"Nah, I'm good. Being surrounded by my family is enough warmth for me." He butted his shoulder against her.

"You're a goof." She butted him back.

When Rhiannon had finally settled down from the thrill of having received two dolls, they moved on to the last two gifts, the packages from her mother.

"I thought Evil Evelyn sent money," Billy said as Devin tore the paper off the erector set her mother had shipped from Savannah.

"I told you. She sent money for us, which I modeled for you last night. For the kids, she picked out presents this year." Watching Devin's eyes light up, Kate had to admit that so far, her mother had done well in the gift department. Billy's eyes had held a similar glow when he saw what her mother's money had bought.

Billy pulled the last present out from under the tree and handed it to Rhiannon.

"Here you go, sweetie, last one. This one's from Endora."

Kate shot him a look and elbowed him in the ribs. "It's from Grandma Evelyn."

Reluctantly, Rhiannon set down her two dolls and began opening her last gift.

"What is it?" Billy leaned toward Kate.

"I have no idea. When we called her on Thanksgiving she asked them what they wanted, but I warned her that they'd change their mind with each television commercial. Which they did, other than Rhiannon and that darn do—"

Rhiannon's scream might have actually pierced her eardrum.

"Look! Look what Grandma sent me!"

"You have got to be shitting me," Billy said.

"This one looks like you, Mommy!"

Kate blinked. The American Girl doll her mother had sent had dark brown hair and green eyes.

"I don't know what to say," she mumbled.

"Holy fuck," Billy whispered, saying exactly what she was thinking.

"Wow, Ree, you kinda hit the jackpot there, didn't you?"

But her daughter wasn't listening, she was tearing through the other items in the box, which included clothing and accessories.

"At least American Girl Kate has a change of clothes," Billy said.

"I'm stunned," Kate said, standing and gathering up the discarded paper and shoving it into a large trash bag. "Not only that she actually bought them things they'd asked for, but that she selected a doll that looks like me."

"Think she's trying to mess with your head?"

"Who knows with my mother? As long as Rhiannon likes it, that's all that matters, right? Although three dolls when she was told not to expect even one goes a long way to undermining our parenting."

Billy shoved the rest of the wrapping paper into the bag and took it from her. "It's Christmas. Long as the kids are happy, who cares? And it's not like she's spoiled or anything. Right?"

"I guess," Kate mumbled, although she couldn't help but wonder if the next time she told her daughter she couldn't have her way, this wouldn't come back to bite her in the ass.

CHAPTER 25

"Can I go out and play T-ball?"

"There's snow outside, dummy."

"Hey!" Billy glared at his daughter from where he leaned against the kitchen counter, sucking down coffee like there was about to be a shortage. "You don't talk to your brother like that."

Kate rolled her eyes at him from where she stood at the stove, squirting pancake batter onto her skillet in the shape of a reindeer. "That's exactly how she talks to her brother," she mouthed.

"But he's being stupid."

"That's enough," said Kate, plopping a maraschino cherry on the reindeer on Devin's plate. "Here's Rudolph's nose. Take your plate and be careful not to drop it."

She handed Billy his plate.

"Don't I get a cherry nose for my reindeer?"

"For making it home for Christmas and surprising us, you get two."

He leaned close enough to brush his lips against her ear. "Can I trade it for something else?"

She snatched the second cherry from his plate and popped it in her mouth. "Absolutely."

"Dev, follow Daddy into the living room. We'll eat by the fireplace, okay? I'll bring your hot cocoa in a minute."

Billy got Devin and Rhiannon settled around the coffee table just as Kate entered, carrying a tray holding her plate, her mug of coffee, and two mugs of cocoa. She set Devin's mug before him.

"Where's my marshmallows?" he cried.

"Sorry, bud."

Billy stood. "I'll go."

"There's an unopened bag in the pantry," Kate called after him. "And you might as well grab the whipped cream from the fridge."

All this sugar and he was pretty sure no one would be taking a nap that afternoon, least of all him. Of course, he'd been away so much over the past year, maybe the kids didn't even take naps anymore.

He was rooting around in the pantry for the marshmallows, when he heard a loud rap on the front door, followed by several more. The clock on the mantel said it was just a little before ten. Marty and Eileen would have left for the airport by now, and Joey was in Hawaii.

Who the hell would show up unannounced this early on Christmas morning?

Billy unlocked the front door and opened it to find a man standing on the porch, holding a huge poinsettia and a box wrapped in Christmas paper. The guy must get paid pretty damn well to deliver on Christmas day; which would explain the Camaro convertible sitting in his driveway. The sucker would probably expect a huge tip.

Bitter cold air seeped in through the screen, hitting Billy in the chest and making him regret not taking advantage of the matching top to his pajamas.

As he pushed open the screen door, the deliveryman turned.

"Hey, man. C'mon in. It's fucking freezing."

"Uh . . ."

"Is that for Katie?"

Looking confused, the man glanced at the plant, then back up at Billy and blinked.

"Uh . . ."

Billy laughed. "Yeah. You said that."

"Hey," Kate called from behind him. "What's taking you so long? Devin's about to have a meltdown because he doesn't have any marsh—Digger!"

Billy glanced at Kate then back at the man standing on his porch. He was no longer freezing. In fact, he was heating up pretty damn fast.

"Digger?" he asked.

Kate's eyes were wide.

Digger. The cop. The one who'd had a huge crush on Kate in high school, and if he were a betting man, the same cop who'd been standing on his front porch last night, offering to come over and help himself to Billy's wife once his children had gone to bed.

"You want to tell me what the fuck is going on?"

Kate looked as if she might be sick. "I have no idea. Digger?"

"I, uh—"

"You said that already, dude. Three times. Either you're moonlighting for the local florist, or you got some explaining to do." He glared down at Kate. "You too."

"Me?" she cried. "What did I do?"

Fuck! He needed to reel in his temper, at least where Kate was concerned. He put his arm around her shoulder. "Nothing. I'm sorry. I didn't mean it the way it came out. Is this the guy who was here last night?"

She nodded.

He pulled her closer, tucking her tight under his arm and turned back to Digger. "Dude. What the fuck?"

His back and forth with Kate must have given the cop a chance to regroup. He didn't seem as ready to bolt as he had when he first realized it had been Billy who had opened the door.

"I just wanted to check on Kate. Make sure she was okay. I understood she and the kids would be alone, and since it was Christmas, I just wanted to let her know I was thinking of her."

"Wrong answer."

Kate must have felt the tension of his body because she gripped the waistband of his pajama bottoms in her hand and tugged.

"Billy." Her voice was low, but the warning note was loud and clear.

"Thank you, Digger," Kate said, although what he really wanted was for her to go back into the living room and leave him to handle it. She didn't, of course.

"I appreciate your concern, but I'm fine, as you can see. And I'm also fine when Billy's working, so there's really no need to check on me, as a police officer or as a friend. As I told you last night, if I'm ever in need of assistance, I know enough to dial 9-1-1."

Kate's response was polite and kind. Typical for her. He, on the other hand, would have preferred to just give him one quick shot to make sure he understood he was barking up the wrong tree—his tree!

And then, as if the bastard hadn't pushed his buttons enough yet, he held out the poinsettia and the package. "These are for you," he said, handing them off to Kate. "Might as well take them."

"Are you fu—"

"Thank you." Kate accepted the offerings, which set Billy's teeth on edge. "Merry Christmas, Digger." As she stepped back, Billy slammed the door shut. He kept his eyes glued on the bastard, hoping to make him realize that he'd be in deep shit if he tried something like this again.

After the door closed, Billy yanked the plant and the box out of Kate's hands, walked to the back door, and hurled them out into the snow. Maybe he was overreacting. Or maybe he didn't get enough sleep. But just the thought of this guy coming around when he wasn't home had him seeing red. And what if Rafe hadn't stepped off that stage and broken his leg? Would this guy be sitting in front of Billy's Christmas tree, eating his reindeer pancakes? It's not that he didn't trust Kate, but it would be just like her to invite him in if she felt sorry for him.

Bastard.

He stalked through the kitchen to find Kate waiting for him in the dining room, her arms folded across her chest and a pissed-off look on her face.

"Was that necessary?"

"Yeah, it fucking was."

She let out a long, low sigh which he'd come to recognize as her pressure release valve. Of the two of them, he probably needed it more.

"Billy. You know you have nothing to worry about, right? I ran into Digger a few days ago at the grocery store. If you want to be angry with someone, be angry with my mother. She somehow gave Digger's mother the impression that things weren't too good between us and that you were away from us by choice. I tried to correct him when he came by last night, but I was so surprised, and the kids wanted me, and to be honest, it made me uncomfortable that he'd even stopped by, especially when it seemed he might still be interested in me."

"Might?" He struggled to keep his voice under control. "There's no *might* if he shows up bearing gifts on Christmas morning, and thinking your husband is out of town."

She slammed her palm against her forehead. "Jeez, Billy. It's been what? Seven years since I'd last seen him?"

"I don't care how long it's been. I don't like him sniffing around what's mine."

The expression on her face told him she wasn't exactly flattered by that last comment. It didn't seem possible, but he might have made it worse.

She blinked rapidly. "Sniffing around? Would you like to pee on my leg? This way Digger, or anyone else who comes sniffing around, will know I'm marked."

Might as well go all in.

"Hopefully that won't be necessary. I think he got the hint, but if I have to, I will. And when I'm done, I'll beat the shit out of him."

"You're a piece of work, you know that?"

"I'll take that as a compliment."

Her eyes narrowed. "Don't."

There was only one way to fix this before he tanked her mood for the rest of the day. He stretched out his fingers, wiggling them, and took a half step toward her.

Her eyes widened. "Don't even think about it."

Crouching, he took another step, reaching for her, his fingers wiggling, threatening. He knew all her most sensitive spots, especially the one at the apex of her hips and thighs.

"No!"

She was trying to look threatening, but her voice broke and the light in her eyes was clearly visible. She hated being tickled, but that was much better than having her hating his caveman-like behavior. Because when it came to protecting what was his—Yeah. His—he'd be a caveman every fucking time.

"C'mon, Katie, you know you can't run from me."

Didn't mean she wouldn't try. She faked to the right, but he was on to her. He caught her just as her bare foot hit the second stair. Wrapping one arm around her waist and the other free to bring her into submission, he tackled her on the stairs. She wiggled fruitlessly as he easily slipped his hand into the elastic waistband of her pajama bottoms.

He nipped at her ear lobe. "You keep rubbing that ass against me and I'm taking you right here on the stairs." He hadn't even started to tickle her and she was already laughing.

"The kids!" she choked out.

"What about 'em? They're too wrapped up in what Santa brought them to come to your rescue."

He went in for the kill, tickling her most sensitive area, while drawing his teeth over the curve of her neck. Damn if he wasn't hard as a rock.

"Keep wiggling, Katie. I might get off just like this."

Or not. The thunder of little feet pounded down the hall.

"Tickle fight!" Devin yelled, hurling himself at Billy's legs. And damn if the little shit didn't start tickling his feet. Rhiannon went for his bare waist, while Kate, still pinned beneath him, yelled "Help!" breathlessly, still squirming to get away.

Billy let go and whipped around, reaching for his son, who was almost as ticklish as his mother. As he grabbed him, Devin went boneless, while Rhiannon, Daddy's little girl, picked up where he left off and started tickling her mother.

So between the screams of laughter and writhing mass of bodies against the stairs, it was hard to hear the steady pounding coming from the kitchen.

"Wait," Kate said, trying to catch her breath. "Is someone knocking?"

Billy stopped as well, trying to listen over Devin's squeals as his sister turned her attention to him.

"I'll fucking kill him," he muttered under his breath, storming toward the back door. Digger was either stupid or had some kind of death wish.

Kate's arm landed on his. "Let me get it."

He glared down at her. "Katie, I swear to God—"

The door popped open and a rush of cold air preceded their visitor. "Hey! I'm freezing my kahunas off out there!"

"Joey?" Kate said.

"Uncle Joey!" No longer interested in tormenting her brother, Rhiannon darted toward the back door, followed by Kate and Devin.

He stomped up the back steps, arms laden with brightly colored packages. He stopped when he saw Billy. "What the hell are you doing here?"

"I live here. What the hell are you doing here?"

"I thought you were in Hawaii," Kate interjected, trying her damnedest to hug him without knocking everything out of his arms.

Joey dumped his load on the kitchen counter. "I didn't go. I couldn't stand the thought of you being alone for Christmas, so I cancelled my trip. I wanted to surprise you." He lowered his voice. "Besides, James was being a dick, and not the good kind."

Kate poked him in the ribs. "Joey." Her voice carried a note of warning.

"Like they'd have a clue. I bet the rock star doesn't even get it." He glowered at Billy.

"Trust me," Billy answered. "I know a dick when I see one."

A loud, frustrated sigh from Kate was enough to warn him off. It seemed Joey got the message as well—almost.

"Anyway, here I am. Another vacation ruined for no reason."

"I'm sorry," Kate said, pulling him in for a long hug.

While Billy had been ready for a throw down with Digger for sniffing around his wife, it was hard not to smile seeing her wrapped in Joey's arms. For as much as the motherfucker irritated the piss out of him, knowing how much Joey loved Kate and how no matter what, he was always there for her, and his kids, was strangely comforting.

When he'd finished with Kate, and taken a turn each with Devin and Rhiannon, Joey stood and assessed the kitchen. "And of course, the more I thought about your Christmas ham and those candied sweet potatoes, I knew there was a reason I'd been avoiding carbs all month." He pulled open the oven, which was empty, and frowned. "Speaking of which—

Kate gasped and her face fell. "Oh no!" She looked from Joey to Billy and back again.

"There is no ham or sweet potatoes. Or scalloped corn, either."

For a boy who grew up with very little in the way of tradition, other than regular beatings at the hands of his father, and disappointments from his mother, Billy had latched on to the ones he and Kate had developed during the short time they'd been married. And ham, candied sweet potatoes, and scalloped corn for Christmas had been one of them.

She chewed nervously on her bottom lip. "Since we were going to officially celebrate Christmas when you came home, I didn't bother to pick up the ham." She looked at Joey. "And I didn't expect to see you today, either."

"So what were you going to make for dinner?" Joey asked.

Her voice was practically a squeak. "Hot dogs."

"For Christmas?"

She shrugged. "I was making what the kids like. Hot dogs. Macaroni and cheese. Chicken fingers."

"Well, hell," Joey said. "You told me that. Maybe subliminally I picked a fight with James just to get my hands on that mac 'n cheese." Joey rubbed his belly, probably trying to make Kate feel better. Which was exactly what Billy needed to do. He pulled her against him.

"You're a wonderful mother, and the way you take care of our kids makes me love you even more." He pressed a kiss on her forehead. "Plus, I love your mac 'n cheese almost as much as I love you."

Her eyes were still shiny, but she laughed. "Okay you two. It's getting a little deep in here."

"More presents!" Devin cried from the kitchen, having spotted Joey's cache on the kitchen counter. "Uncle Joey brought presents!"

Joey spun around. "Of course Uncle Joey brought presents," he said, sounding like he was scolding them for being surprised. "And I think we should open them right now, and then you can show me what Santa brought you."

The kids charged down the hall, into the living room, while Joey gathered his packages.

"I hope you didn't overdo it," Kate said, following him.

"I plead the fifth," he said, his voice at first moderated, but then he clapped his hands and squealed. "But I did get her that doll she wanted, the American Girl one? I can't wait to see how excited she is to open it."

Kate froze as Joey dashed down the hall after Devin and Rhiannon, yelling as loudly as they were.

She looked up at Billy. "That's four dolls. I told her she couldn't have even one. Do you think we should tell him not give it to her? Maybe he could just tell her what he bought for her hadn't come in yet, and he can give her something else?"

"No, why would you do that?"

"Because, Billy, that's four dolls. Four very expensive dolls."

He shrugged. "So."

"So? Don't you think she's going to expect that because she wants something, she's going to get it? I don't want her to get spoiled."

"C'mon, Katie. Spoiled? That'll never happen."

Rhiannon's scream of surprise reached them from the other side of the house.

Kate looked up at him, shaking her head.

"I hope you're right."

⁓

Devin was delighted with the train set Joey had given him, and Billy seemed equally enthralled with his 18-year-old bottle of Scotch. Now it was Kate's turn.

Joey settled a large box in her lap and a smaller one beside her on the sofa. Both were elaborately decorated in a thick, navy paper stamped with gold stars, navy satin ribbon and accented with clusters of gold bells.

She fingered the shiny ribbon. "Judging by the wrapping alone, this looks really expensive, Joey."

"Don't worry about it. Just open it." He was practically bouncing.

Kate slipped the ribbon off. She wanted to keep it, as well as the gorgeous paper.

"Oh for crying out loud! Just tear it off."

She deflected Joey's hand in time to keep him from ripping the paper. Billy sat on the floor beside her with Devin in his lap.

"I thought you knew her better than that," he said to Joey. "She's tried to reuse fancy wrapping paper as long as I've known her. It's a throwback to Evelyn."

They could tease her all they wanted. She was saving the paper. It was too beautiful to rip apart and throw away. Knowing how itchy it was making Joey to watch her, she took her time, smoothing the paper into neat folds once she'd lifted it from the box and biting her lip the entire time to keep from laughing at his impatience.

He folded his arms and glared at her. "Are you about finished there?"

She couldn't hold back anymore. "Yes," she said, going all in and tearing the top off the box.

Crisp white tissue paper, sealed with a gold foil medallion didn't require the care she'd given to the wrapping paper, so she tore it open to find what looked like a puddle of liquid gold. She ran her fingers over the fabric. It was cool and silky and just about the softest thing she'd ever touched.

"Hold it up," Joey said, nudging her.

It was a scrap of a dress, really. If it was more than two yards of fabric, she'd be surprised, but it was gorgeous.

Billy's response was a long, low whistle. "Whoa, babe. You will look amazing in that."

She held the dress up against her chest, covering her red plaid pajamas, which were much more her speed.

"It's beautiful, Joey. But where would I ever wear something like this?"

He pushed the second, smaller box toward her. "Um, New Year's Eve? Remember?"

Billy answered before she could. "The New Year's gig in New York is up in the air. And even if it happens, since Evelyn bailed on us, we've got no one to watch the kids, so Katie couldn't go anyway."

Joey, who'd been kneeling in front of her while she opened his presents, sat back on his haunches with a loud huff. "And what am I? Chopped liver?"

She and Billy exchanged glances and she laughed. "Seriously? You hate coming to Belleville. Now you're offering to come back in a week instead of ringing in the new year at some swanky party so that you can spend it babysitting?" She shook her head. "C'mon, Joey. I couldn't ask you to do that."

"You're not asking. I'm offering."

She'd known him since the third grade, and the look on his face told her he was sincere. But still.

"That's sweet of you, but like Billy said, the gig will probably be cancelled—"

"Even better." He stood and brushed imaginary dirt from the knees of his designer jeans. "One of my clients offered me two tickets to the Marriott Marquis for New Year's Eve. They're yours. You and the rock star can go. I'll come back Friday and you two can spend the weekend in New York. Stay at my apartment. I mean it, Kate. Let me do this for you. It will make what I have to tell you next a lot easier."

Now Joey looked worried. He was even chewing on his lip, which made her heart sink. Was he sick? Moving to L.A.?

She tried to swallow the sudden lump in her throat. "What is it?"

He held up the unopened box, set it in her lap, and tapped on it.

"There's a pair of Manolo stilettos in here—"

"Joey!"

He held up his hand. "Relax. They're borrowed. I have a friend who works at Vogue. They have to go back. But the dress is yours."

She was either going to hit him or hug him.

"Is that the bad news? That I can't keep a pair of shoes I have no business owning in the first place?"

He nodded warily, and Kate slumped with relief.

"Jeez. You can be so overly dramatic sometimes, you know that?"

"Sometimes?" Billy muttered.

Joey shot him a dark look, but before he could respond, Rhiannon interrupted.

"Uncle Joey? Could you give my doll an updo?"

Kate rolled her eyes at Billy. They had the only six-year-old in New Jersey who knew what an updo was.

"An updo? I don't see why not." Joey settled himself on the floor next to Rhiannon. "How about a French twist? We'll get her all dolled up for New Year's Eve." He nudged Rhiannon in the ribs with his elbow. "Get it? Dolled up?"

She stared at him blankly.

"Everyone's a critic in this house. Go find me a brush and some bobby pins and I'll see what I can do."

Rhiannon scrambled to her feet and took off running. Joey began fiddling with the doll's hair, while Devin dumped about a million Lego pieces onto the floor.

"Remind me not to go barefoot again," she said to Billy as she piled the breakfast dishes onto her tray and carried it into the kitchen. Billy followed with the overflow.

"Well?" he asked as she turned on the hot water and squirted in some dish liquid. "What do you think?"

"About what?"

"About Joey's offer."

She shook her head. "I can't ask him to watch the kids for three days. That's crazy."

"You're not asking. He's offering. He even said that."

It was tempting, and she certainly trusted Joey with the kids. It was just too much to ask.

"And what about the dress?"

"What about it?"

He wrapped his arms around her waist and rested his chin on her shoulder. "I want to see you in that dress."

"I'll model it for you later."

"C'mon, Kate. Say yes. Please."

"Billy—"

Suds flew up in the air as he spun her around. Bubbles floated around them.

"Listen. I've been miserable these past few weeks without you. And who knows how soon I'll be back on tour. Please do this for me. Please, Katie. A couple days alone with you. We've never been apart on New Year's Eve since we met, and if the gig isn't cancelled, that's what's going to happen. I don't want to be without you for New Year's, Katie."

"I don't want that either—"

His eyes locked on hers, pleading. "Then say yes."

He was right. The past few weeks had been hard on both of them this time, but even worse for him. It had always been hard for her to say no to him, and why should she? Especially when what he was asking for was time alone with each other.

She lifted her hands and tucked the golden strands of hair behind his ears. "Yes."

He grinned, and just like always, her knees grew weak and her pulse raced. When he kissed her like they were the only two people in the house, it was a good thing his arms were wrapped around her waist. He pulled away only enough to run his nose along her jaw, up to her ear.

"Dance with me, Katie."

"Always, Billy."

The End

ACKNOWLEDGEMENTS

When I finished writing *All I Ever Wanted*, I thought that was the end of Billy and Kate's story, even though I didn't want to say goodbye. I was thinking someday I might write Rhiannon's story, or maybe Devin's, but I wanted to let Billy and Kate get on with their lives without me poking around in their business. But then, just before *All I Ever Wanted* was published, I saw an image of model Sean Brandon, taken by Logan Noh, and I thought, "Damn, he looks like my Billy."

A tiny seed was planted. I watered it a bit and let it germinate until a story began to grow. When it was ready, I turned to my wonderful critique partners, David L. Williams, Gretchen Anthony, and Laura Broullire, whose spot-on suggestions helped me create one more story for Billy and Kate.

And since Sean was my inspiration, I tracked down Logan Noh and was thrilled when he allowed me to use Sean's picture on the cover of this book.

Of course I have to thank Lori Ryser, who doubled down on this book, taking on the dual role of line editing and proofreading. I don't know that I can ever thank her enough for all she's done for me. I'm going to hug her so hard one of these days.

There are a few more people I'd like to thank.

Whitney Barbetti: You are one of my favorite authors and one of my favorite people. I would be lost without you. You are kind, and talented, and generous.

Karla Sorensen: Thank you for polishing my back cover copy—again. (And thanks for keeping me entertained with your wonderful books.)

Jena Camp: Thanks for all your help promoting my books and for creating the most gorgeous teasers.

Sound engineer and tour manager Carlos Novais: Thank you for answering my questions about tour life. You have one of the best jobs in rock 'n' roll, and you're a hell of a nice guy too. I hope you don't mind that I named my tour manager after you.

Airline pilot Matt Johnson: Thanks for being engaged to my friend Aimee Casper and educating me on Gulfstreams and airports, and for even remembering LAX back in the '90s. And Aimee, thanks for your love and support and for connecting me with Matt.

JudiRae Kesner: Thank you for all your wonderful name suggestions. Rafe Summerland is all yours, babe.

Garrett Cimms: You always make your mama proud, especially when you design such beautiful covers.

And lastly, much love and gratitude to my husband, Jim. I couldn't write a single word without you.

ABOUT THE AUTHOR

Karen Cimms is a writer, editor, and music lover. She was born and raised in New Jersey and still thinks of the Garden State as home. She began her career at an early age rewriting the endings to her favorite books. It was a mostly unsuccessful endeavor, but she likes to think she invented fanfiction. Karen is a lifelong Jersey corn enthusiast, and is obsessed with (in no particular order) books, shoes, dishes, and Brad Pitt. In her spare time she likes to quilt, decorate, and entertain. Just kidding–she has no spare time. Although she's fond of certain pigeons, she is terrified of pet birds, scary movies and Mr. Peanut.

Karen is married to her favorite lead guitar player. Her children enjoy tormenting her with countless mean-spirited pranks because they love her. She currently lives in Northeast Pennsylvania, although her heart is usually in Maine.

ALSO BY KAREN CIMMS

Of Love and Madness Series

At This Moment (Book 1)
We All Fall Down (Book 2)
All I Ever Wanted (Book 3)
You're All I Want for Christmas (Novella)

For updates on new releases, please visit www.karencimms.com.

I THE GUY
HISTORIAN'S
JOURNAL

howdy!

I WRITE
ACTION
ADVENTURE

The Bryan Museum
the Romance of The West

iWRITE
IWRITE.ORG

TEXAS & THE AMERICAN WEST

Written by Melissa M. Williams
Illustrated by Ryan Shaw

Printed using Dyslexie Font.
Visit dyslexiefont.com.